# THE DUKE WHO RUINED CHRISTMAS

## CHRISTMAS DUKES
### BOOK TWO

## SCARLETT SCOTT

*The Duke Who Ruined Christmas*

Christmas Dukes Book 2

All rights reserved.

Copyright © 2025 by Scarlett Scott™

Published by Happily Ever After Books, LLC

Edited by Grace Bradley and Lisa Hollett, Silently Correcting Your Grammar

Cover Design by EDH Professionals

This book or any portion thereof may not be reproduced or used in any manner whatsoever without the express written permission of the publisher except for the use of brief quotations in a book review.

The unauthorized reproduction or distribution of this copyrighted work is illegal. No part of this book may be scanned, uploaded, or distributed via the Internet or any other means, electronic or print, without the publisher's permission. Criminal copyright infringement, including infringement without monetary gain, is punishable by law.

This book is a work of fiction and any resemblance to persons, living or dead, or places, events, or locales, is purely coincidental. The characters are productions of the author's imagination and used fictitiously.

Scarlett Scott™ is a registered trademark of Happily Ever After Books, LLC.

For more information, contact author Scarlett Scott™.

https://scarlettscottauthor.com/

*For my mom and my sister~
Thank you for Nanny's Summer Camp so I could write all the words.*

# CHAPTER 1

YORKSHIRE, ENGLAND

*December 1885*

The Duke of Marchingham was an arrogant, haughty arse.

And Miss Adelia Fox of New York City, sole daughter of the ridiculously wealthy railroad magnate Cornelius Fox, had every intention of informing the intolerable fellow of that.

Supposing she didn't freeze to death in a Yorkshire snow bank first.

Unfortunately, the likelihood of her imminent demise was growing stronger with each passing minute that she remained alone with a sea of her trunks in the midst of only heaven knew where. She sighed heavily as she peeked through the frigid carriage's Venetian blinds. A wall of white descended from the leaden sky, giving no indication it would cease any time soon.

Sending their coachman Alfred and Aunt Pearl ahead of

her with Dandy had been her only choice. With the overloaded carriage mired firmly in the snow and unable to move, and the manor house to which they were traveling nowhere in sight, she'd been forced to act. Poor Dandy would have frozen by now.

Still, reaching an untimely end in the wilds of England was decidedly not the manner in which Addy had planned to spend the Christmas season. Rather, she had intended to surprise her dearest friends from the Swiss finishing school she'd been forced to attend at her mother's determined insistence. Mama was intent upon Addy finding a proper husband—the nobler, the better, a foreign prince if possible. Addy, meanwhile, was equally intent upon never surrendering her freedom to the institution—and particularly not with some dreadful foreign prince.

As she'd predicted, finishing school had proven deadly dull. Addy had done everything in her power to be sent home. Only two good things had come of the decidedly miserable experience. The first had been the friendship she'd forged with Lady Lila and Lady Violetta "Letty" Hawthorne. And the second was her beloved French bulldog, Dandelion. After discovering her at a stop in Paris, Addy had brought Dandy home to New York City with her, and they'd been inseparable ever since.

Lady Letty and Lady Lila, however, had returned to England following their equally ignominious tenure at Académie Clairemont. And oh, how dearly she'd missed them over the past three years. It was difficult to believe how much time had passed since Addy had been sent away from finishing school in disgrace herself.

They'd been relegated to long-winded letters and the occasional transatlantic telegram in the intervening years. But it had been a pale comparison to the times they had spent laughing and singing and plotting their latest foibles together in Switzerland. Finally, they were meant to have been reunited, *Les Trois Mousquetaires*, as they had been known at the Académie Clairemont. And only because Addy had decided she'd had enough of their elder brother's infuriating refusal to allow them to visit her in New York City.

This time, she had chosen to surprise her friends. When they had written to her with grave disappointment at their inability to accept her invitation for a Christmas in New York City thanks to the duke's maddening disapproval, Addy had decided it was time to take matters into her own hands.

Mama had been thrilled. Addy's trip to England—and to a duke's manor house, no less—was a feather in her cap and a source of unabashed bragging to her inner circle.

"Only think of how fortunate the Duke of Marchingham will be to have my Adelia paying him a call," she had told Mrs. William Spencer Clay with a smug air. "I can just imagine how utterly charmed such a gentleman will be by darling Adelia's clever wit."

*Darling Adelia* was something Mama only called her in public. The rest of the time, she was more commonly referred to as *Adelia Louise Stonehurst Fox* in an irate fashion. Mama was quite fond of reminding everyone she'd been born a Stonehurst. Even when she was enraged.

For her part, Mrs. William Spencer Clay had mustered up a smile that had more resembled a grimace of despair, for she had four daughters of her own, none of whom had been invited to spend Christmas with a duke. "Of course, my dear Bettina."

Never mind that Addy hadn't been invited either.

With another sigh, she released her hold on the blinds, allowing them to close and blot out the unrelenting snowy vista beyond. Her fingers were numb inside her gloves, so she tucked them beneath the furs in her lap.

Perhaps her end would be fitting. Mama had forever

lectured her that she needed to be more judicious in her decisions. And as much as Addy despised conceding any point to her mother, however small, as she shivered in misery in the carriage that had failed on the final leg of her journey, she had to admit that perhaps Mama had been right after all...

*Thump, thump, thump.*

Addy screamed. Then she jolted upright in her seat with so much force, propelled by her startlement, that she struck her head on the carriage roof.

Her scream died in a cry of distress.

*Thump, thump, thump, thump, thump.*

The angry raps on the carriage door had nearly doubled. And they were growing louder.

"Are you in there, madam?"

The deep, masculine voice was accented and unfamiliar. Not Alfred. Oh dear. Surely Alfred would have returned with whatever help he had managed to find. He would never dare to abandon Addy's side. Not unless she had ordered him to, which she had only done so that the most vulnerable members of their party might be spared.

What if the man at her carriage door was an opportunistic thief who had spied her stranded carriage and all its trunks? What if his intention was to rob her?

Her first instinct was to avoid answering. She held her breath and her tongue, pressing her back to the squabs and not daring to move.

Addy reached a gloved hand toward her favorite diamond earrings as she kept her stare fixed upon the door.

"Madam?"

Perhaps she ought to let him rob her in exchange for getting her to the nearest fireplace so that she could warm herself. She flexed her toes in her silk boots. They, too, were icy and numb.

*Thump, thump.*

"The door is frozen shut. Stand back. I'm going to have to break it down to reach you."

So that was why the man was beating on the carriage.

The warning spurred her to action. Addy held up a hand. "Wait. Don't break down the d—"

Her words were swallowed by the splintering crack as the carriage door thundered open.

"Door," she finished lamely as she stared at the irate man who had just crashed into her carriage, broad shoulder first.

A frenzied burst of snow puffed around him, making him seem, for a brief moment, otherworldly. His hat had been knocked from his head, revealing thick, golden waves. His jaw was strong, leading to a cleft chin and lips that were as forbidding as they were inviting. His cheekbones were prominent blades, his forehead was high, and he possessed more beauty than she'd ever seen in a man. His form was large and strong, and he was tall beneath the snow-flecked greatcoat he wore.

He stole Addy's breath. Or no, perhaps that was the cold bursting in from the outdoors, making it difficult to inflate her lungs, forcing her heart to beat fast and hard.

Pinning her with a glacial blue glare, he extended a hand. "Come."

She eyed his hand as if it were a bear trap. "I don't think so, sir."

He regarded her, his demeanor brooding. "You have somewhere else to be in this maelstrom?"

"Yes," she snapped back, nettled by his smug air. "That is why I'm in a carriage."

A lone, golden eyebrow winged upward. "A carriage that is stuck in a snowbank. I doubt it's capable of conveying you anywhere for the foreseeable future."

Well, damn him for mentioning it.

He wasn't wrong, of course. But she had no wish to feel as if she were easy prey for this strapping stranger who had come upon her.

"Have you passed anyone on the road?" she asked, thinking of Alfred, Aunt Pearl, and Dandy.

If anything ill had befallen them before they had reached Marchingham Hall…

No, she refused to think it.

"I daresay no one else is stupid enough to venture into a snowstorm at present," he drawled.

His uncharitable response instantly drew her ire. "Are you insinuating I'm lacking in intelligence, sir?"

Her mind whirled. Perhaps that meant Alfred, Aunt Pearl, and Dandy had made it to Marchingham Hall. She hoped and prayed that was the case. They'd taken the horses at her insistence, leaving Addy with her trunks. Someone had to guard her belongings. She couldn't simply abandon them to the road.

"I am not insinuating anything, madam," the man said, his tone biting.

Of course it would be just Addy's peculiar brand of fortune to find herself being robbed in the midst of a snowstorm by the most insolent, dreadful man she'd ever met. Still, she needed his help. Perhaps he could be persuaded to aid her without resorting to nefarious means.

"Take my earrings," she said suddenly, reaching for them both with gloved hands. "They're diamond and worth quite a bit. They'll fetch you more than enough if you're willing to take me somewhere safe and warm until this infernal storm passes."

Unfortunately, her frozen fingers and the impractical kidskin rendered it impossible for her to remove either earring.

He watched her, his stare unnerving. "Get out of the carriage."

His tone was icy and brusque.

"You needn't be so rude, sir," she chastised him.

"Out," he commanded again in a cold, clipped voice.

She took umbrage at that voice. If he had dared to speak to her thus back home in New York City, why, she would have had him thrown out on his ear. Addy looked over his shoulder at the swirling snow. Pity there was nowhere to throw him now.

"You ought to address a lady with respect," she returned primly. "Has no one ever taught you manners? But then, I suppose if they had, you wouldn't have to resort to robbing carriages to earn your bread."

He blinked and then stared at her as if she had just turned into something mysterious and perplexing before him.

And then his brow furrowed, and he gave her the most ferocious glare she'd ever experienced in her nearly twenty-three years.

"You think I'm robbing your carriage." He stated it as a grim fact.

Wasn't he?

A gust of wind sent a fresh rush of snowflakes tumbling into the carriage.

Addy shivered. "Yes, of course that's what I think. Why else would you break down the carriage door and demand I get out of it?"

"Because," he said slowly and with agonizing precision, "the door was frozen shut. As I already explained. Now, if you please, get out of the blasted carriage. My hat is on the ground, filling with snow, this storm shows no inclination of stopping, and I would prefer not to perish by turning into a block of ice."

Sarcasm dripped from his words. Apparently, her speech

about manners had fallen upon ears that were decidedly uninterested in listening.

She glanced back to his outstretched hand. "Where do you intend to take me?"

"To Marchingham Hall," he growled. "Where else?"

"How opportune." She grudgingly laid her gloved hand in his. "That is my intended destination."

His fingers closed over hers, and he pulled her unceremoniously from the carriage. His motions were so swift and strong that she nearly went headlong into the snow. She stumbled on cold, booted feet, catching herself at the last moment. Snow fell mercilessly upon them.

The stranger had bent to retrieve his hat, which was indeed filling with snow, from the ground. With a sound of irritation, he emptied it and then stuffed it back upon his head.

"Follow me, madam," he said with all the cheer of a pallbearer.

And then he had the temerity to turn his back to her, stalking away to where a massive brown mount awaited. The horse had a patch of white on its face and long white fur on each leg.

"What about my trunks?" she asked, looking over her shoulder to where the abandoned carriage sat helplessly mired, her trunks piled high.

"They'll have to wait," the man said, unconcerned.

Horror struck. "They can't wait! My gowns, my shoes, my jewels! They'll all be stolen or ruined."

He reached the horse and cast a harsh glance in her direction. "Then perhaps you ought to have thought of that before setting out on a journey in a snowstorm."

"But I need them," she protested.

He hissed out an irritated sigh. "Does it look as if I presently have a way to transport your trunks?"

Addy eyed the gargantuan horse. "No."

"Would you care to freeze to death in this snowstorm?"

He was quite beastly, this wretched man. It was on the tip of her tongue to tell him so, but then Addy thought better of it. There was always the chance he would leave her stranded here.

"I would not, sir," she admitted.

"Then get on the horse," he said.

Addy cast another forlorn glance back at her trunks, which were already coated in white. Her precious silks from France. Her shoes. Her sapphires and diamonds and emeralds. Dandy's favorite blanket.

"Now," he snapped when she hesitated.

Addy turned back to the dreadful stranger. "Fine. But only because I have no wish to die in a Yorkshire snowbank."

He grumbled something unpleasant beneath his breath, and she had no doubt it was a vile insult against herself. Ignoring the hand he offered her, she gathered what remained of her shredded pride and heaved herself up into the saddle. It was no easy feat, given the weight of her travel gown and her frozen legs.

He swung up in front of her. "Hold on to me."

She scarcely had her arms wrapped awkwardly around his lean torso before he kicked the horse into a gallop. They were off down the road, snow pelting them, leaving the carriage and her worldly possessions behind.

By the time Lion reached Marchingham Hall, he was frozen, surly, and more vexed with Miss Adelia Fox than he could recall being with anyone he'd ever known.

The woman was a bloody menace in silk skirts.

A spoiled, outrageous hoyden who had mistaken him for a common footpad.

And most of all, she was an uninvited guest who had unexpectedly arrived at his manor house in the midst of a vicious snowstorm with half of New York City and a mad dog in tow. She was damned fortunate the elderly manservant, maiden aunt, and mongrel she had brought with her for accompaniment had made it to his door. Otherwise, the lot of them would have been icicles by morning.

"Where have you taken me?" she demanded, her American accent strangely pleasant.

It aggrieved him mightily that he found her voice mellifluous. He was meant to find all qualities concerning Miss Fox deeply, unutterably repellent.

"Welcome to Marchingham Hall," he told the infuriating woman as he drew Athena to a halt before the front portico.

If his voice was laced with sarcasm, then so be it. He had never intended to play host to her.

"*This* is Marchingham Hall?"

Surely he didn't denote a trace of disbelief in her voice? Lion was more than aware that the extensive manor house, most of which had been built in the seventeenth and eighteenth centuries, was in varying states of disrepair. But how dare she look down her nose upon his ancestral dwelling?

"Are you hard of hearing, madam?" he snapped.

The maddening Miss Fox, whose arms were yet wrapped about his midsection and whose breasts had occasionally and quite scandalously grazed his person during their snowy journey, made an indelicate snort.

"Of course not. I was merely expecting something less… old, I suppose."

*Less old.*

He ought to have left the mannerless American chit to her fate in that frigid carriage.

"You may release me now so that I can dismount," he informed her icily. "Unless you wish to remain in the snow whilst you heap insults upon one of the finest examples of Palladian architecture in England."

She withdrew her arms. "Forgive me. Mama always says my tongue is faster than my mind. I speak without thought."

"I'm sure that's the least concerning observation your mother might have made about you," he muttered as he dismounted, his booted feet landing in powdery snow.

His head groom emerged from the equally dilapidated stables, approaching through the snow to return Athena to the haven of her stall. Whilst some of the edifice needed a new roof, Athena's area remained dry. Come spring, Lion would have to see to as many repairs as the estate could afford. He'd been delaying far too long as it was in the hope he could change the fortunes of Marchingham Hall. Thus far, it had proven a losing battle.

Lion held up a gloved hand for Miss Fox. She was quite pale, snow lining what had been a dashing hat with flowers and feathers, matching her travel pelisse. Her lower lip quivered, her teeth chattering.

He banished a swift rush of sympathy, for she had brought this on herself with her madcap scheming. She was fortunate she hadn't frozen to death in that blasted stuck carriage. She accepted his aid, dismounting stiffly and stumbling into him.

When she collided with his chest, he grasped her waist, steadying her.

"Oh," she exclaimed.

The scent of violets permeated the air. Violets with a hint of orris root. He'd caught absurd little traces of her perfume on the ride to Marchingham Hall.

Her eyes were a truly mesmerizing shade of green, brilliant as spring grass. A snowflake caught on her golden lashes, and her hands were on his shoulders, as if holding him to her in a loving embrace.

"Th-thank you," she said, teeth clicking together.

She needed to get inside and warm herself before a roaring fire. Gently, he settled her away from him. The more distance between the two of them, the better. Ideally, there would yet again be an ocean as soon as possible.

"Your Grace," Jacob greeted him as he approached, tugging at his forelock. "I'll take Athena out of the snow and see her settled."

Lion gave his mount a fond rub on her muzzle and then handed off the reins to the groom. "Thank you, Jacob."

Reluctantly, he turned back to his unwanted guest, offering her his arm. "Miss Fox?"

Her brow wrinkled. "Are you...?"

"The Duke of Marchingham," he informed her, garnering a bit of enjoyment from the shock passing over her face. "Quite."

"Not a thief, then."

"Not a thief."

"Oh."

She bit her lip, and then a shudder went over her as the wind blew snow into their faces. The ridiculous woman almost sounded dismayed. But then, what had he expected from her? A proper curtsy? The appropriate deference that was his due? Hardly. Miss Adelia Fox's reputation preceded her.

"I expect you shall need to stand before the fire and warm yourself," he said. "Come. There's no need to tarry in the snow."

He guided his vexing, unwanted guest beneath the portico where they were at last sheltered from the snow and then to the double doors, which swept open at their approach. Stevens, his loyal butler, bowed and stood back to allow them entrance. Lionel stripped away his gloves, hat, and coat, handing them off.

Suddenly, a small creature raced into the entry hall, barking loudly enough to make Lion wince. The hound rushed directly for Miss Fox, emitting a sound that was more suited to a cat than a dog.

Miss Fox dropped to her knees in a sea of wool and snow. She eagerly scooped the mongrel into her arms, whereupon it proceeded to thoroughly lick her face and ears, knocking her snow-laden hat askew in its vigor.

"Oh, my darling," she was crooning to the pointy-eared hound. "Mama missed you too. Yes, she did. Yes, Mama missed you, sweet pea."

Lion stared at the spectacle of snow and woman and dog on the marble floor. How disgraceful. He wasn't surprised, of course. But he remained properly horrified as the hound proceeded to lick Miss Fox's throat as she giggled in scandalous abandon.

The sound of her laughter wasn't grating as some women's levity was. But it was loud and boisterous, wild peals that echoed off the high ceilings. Stevens clasped his hands behind his back and respectfully averted his gaze. And well he might have done, for Marchingham Hall had presently, and quite literally, gone to the dogs.

Lion needed to act. Posthaste.

"I'm afraid that the mongrel will need to bed down in the stables," he warned Miss Fox, interrupting her reunion.

The hound licked her cheek, and Lion found himself incongruously, ridiculously envious of the brindle dog. He tamped down the unwanted sensation at once.

"She cannot sleep in the stables," Miss Fox said, her voice outraged. "She sleeps with me."

"Then perhaps you shall also seek shelter in the stables," he said.

He didn't mean it, of course. Unfortunately, the dreadful Miss Fox would have to remain under this roof until the snow ceased and the roads to York were passable again. But he'd never had an American writhing on his entryway floor with a dog before.

It was making him peevish.

"You expect me to bed down with your horses?" she asked, looking astonished by such a prospect. "I think not, sir. Where are Letty and Lila? They'll no doubt be horrified to learn of their brother's ill treatment of their closest finishing-school friend."

"By closest friend, do you mean to say the friend whose ruinous, reckless influence caused them to be sent away from finishing school?" he asked sharply. "Because that is the only Miss Adelia Fox I am aware of, a cunning, wayward American jade who encouraged my sisters to make unfortunate decisions with lasting consequences."

She flinched as if he had struck her, and Lion knew a moment of regret for speaking so harshly, particularly before a servant. He sent a pointed glance in the butler's direction, and Stevens caught his gaze, offering a barely perceptible nod before he disappeared.

"You disapprove of me," Miss Fox said, cradling her dog to her bodice now as she eyed Lion as if he were a monster.

"How can I not?"

"I can explain what happened, you know, as can Letty and Lila. Where are they? Are you keeping them locked away somewhere?"

The suspicious glare she pinned him with suggested she thought him capable of all manner of villainy.

"Lady Violetta and Lady Lila are not in residence," he informed her. "They are a day's train ride away, visiting our aunt and uncle, the Earl and Countess of Hargrove."

Her mouth fell open, and for once, the minx was reduced to silence.

"They're not here at Marchingham Hall?" she asked at length.

"As I just said."

"I intended to surprise them."

She looked so heartbroken in that moment, almost comically bereft with her hat halfway off her head, snow still lining her pelisse, and the frenetic dog in her lap. Then she sniffled, tears welling in her vivid green eyes.

Well, Christ.

The woman was mad *and* maudlin. She was also presently melting snow all over his floor whilst seated indecorously upon it.

With an irritated sigh, he stalked forward, extending a hand to her.

The mongrel made a high-pitched sound of outrage and nipped at Lion's fingers.

He glared at the creature. "Do you dare to bite me in my own home, you insolent mongrel?"

"She would never bite anyone," Miss Fox hastily defended the dog in her lap. "Would you, sweet pea?"

The dog licked her chin in response.

Lion knew when he had felt teeth, curse the woman. Fortunately for the hound, she hadn't clamped down or actually caused him injury.

"Regardless, it will need to bed down in the stables," he informed her coolly.

"No." Miss Fox clutched the dog to her.

"Yes. Because this is *my* home, and *I* do not like mongrels."

"Spend some time with her, and you'll change your mind."

He glared.

She smiled brightly.

Lion hissed out a sigh of frustration. "I can assure you that nothing can alter my opinion on the matter."

He'd had a dog once. Mittens had been struck by a cart and killed. Since that wretched day, Lion had been unable to stomach the presence of any dog in his vicinity. This particular one was no different.

"To the stables with the mongrel," he added harshly before adding, "and do get up off the floor, Miss Fox. I understand you are American, but one would imagine you possess at least a modicum of decorum. I'll see that Mrs. Burton comes to show you to your room."

With a curt, hasty bow, he took his leave.

# CHAPTER 2

*A*ddy was finally dry and warm, and she was more convinced than ever that the Duke of Marchingham was indeed an arrogant, haughty arse.

Perhaps worse.

Strike that.

*Definitely* worse.

He was a despot, a supercilious, unkind jackass, and that was simply that. How dare he insist upon her precious darling sleeping in the cold stables? And more importantly, how had two vibrant, wonderful ladies like Lila and Letty been cut from the same cloth as such a terrible man? It defied logic.

Bundled up in a blanket before the merrily crackling fire in the room she'd been given, Dandy in her lap, Addy pressed a kiss to her beloved French bulldog's head. The only way Dandy was sleeping in the cold was if Marchingham pried her from Addy's dead hands.

"I'm thankful the duke found you when he did," Aunt Pearl said from the other wingback chair flanking the hearth.

Like Addy's chair, and like every part of Marchingham

Hall she'd seen thus far, the elegant pieces of furniture were worn. Elegant and clearly of excellent craftsmanship. But in need of loving attention. Despite the exterior clearly in need of repair, she hadn't expected the inside of the manor house to be so shabby.

"Anyone with eyes could have found me," Addy grumbled. "I was sitting in a carriage in the midst of the snow. It isn't as if he committed some manner of impossible feat."

Aunt Pearl tutted. "You could have suffered frostbite, or, heaven forbid, even worse. I never would have forgiven myself if anything ill had befallen you, and I daresay neither would your mother and father."

"I'm persuaded that being forced to rely upon the dubious hospitality of the Duke of Marchingham *is* worse than frostbite," Addy drawled, feeling far from magnanimous where he was concerned.

The man was colder than the wintry snow he had helped her to escape.

He was rude. Conceited. Icy. He had scarcely even deigned to speak to her, apart from issuing edicts. And his response to Dandy had been particularly infuriating.

"You mustn't exhibit such ingratitude, Adelia," Aunt Pearl reprimanded with an uncharacteristic sharpness in her voice. "The duke likely saved your life."

"I could have walked the distance with ease," she sniffed, even though her assertion was far from true.

The carriage had mired in the deep snow a fairly significant distance from the manor house—and by horse. With her impractical skirts and silk boots, she wouldn't have made it far. But the notion that she was somehow indebted to the duke wounded her pride. She refused to accept it.

She didn't like the man.

"I doubt it very much," Aunt Pearl insisted. "When Alfred, Dandy, and I arrived without you and explained we'd left you behind in the carriage with your trunks, he wasted no time in riding out in search of you."

"I'm sure it was with great reluctance," Addy said stubbornly. "I'm surprised he didn't send a servant instead."

"It would seem there is a dearth of domestics here," Aunt Pearl noted. "It's almost as if the manor house is abandoned. The room I've been given was closed up, the furniture all under covers, with a lone maid sent to ready it for my use. However, I do believe His Grace rode off in search of you himself because he wanted to see to your welfare personally. He recognized your name at once."

Addy could only imagine how the conversation had gone. The duke would have been initially confused and then no doubt in a rage. According to Letty and Lila, he blamed Addy for their dismissal from Académie Clairemont. It was the reason he continually refused to allow them to visit her in New York City despite years of invitations.

"I suppose that I *am* rather infamous," she muttered.

Dandy looked up at her, gold-flecked brown eyes adoring. Addy kissed Dandy's head a second time. "Mama is quite well-known, and sometimes for dubious reasons," she crooned. "Yes, she is."

Dandy opened her mouth and then closed it in response.

"I know you don't believe it, darling, but it's true," Addy told Dandy in a singsong voice.

Dandy launched herself at Addy, frantically licking behind her ears. Addy laughed and clutched the muscular pup to her, lest she fall off the chair. Dandy's affection was, like everything else she did, unfailingly exuberant.

"You should know better than to speak to Dandy like that," Aunt Pearl chastised, clicking her tongue. "She gets far too excited."

Addy felt the sharp edge of a tooth on her right ear. "Down, you little scamp. No eating my diamond earrings."

"How are you going to keep her from the duke?" Aunt Pearl asked, frowning. "He was most aggrieved when he spied Dandy at our arrival and only allowed her to remain within until she was warmed with Alfred and me."

"I can imagine." Addy wrestled Dandy back into her lap. "Apparently, he has an aversion to dogs, which also means that he doesn't have a soul. I could have guessed as much, given his treatment of his poor sisters. The duke has the personality of a pile of frozen horse dung."

Dandy's mouth was open wide to reveal her alligator-like teeth as she presented her belly for a rub next. Addy obliged, trying to push all unwelcome thoughts of the Duke of Marchingham from her mind.

"And to think you traveled all the way to Paris to find such a wild dog," Aunt Pearl said.

Addy covered Dandy's silken ears. "She's not wild, and you had better not let her hear you utter such blasphemy either. She's merely high-spirited."

Aunt Pearl chuckled. "Now you sound like your father defending you to your mother when you were a girl getting into all manner of scrapes."

Papa had always been Addy's champion. He spoiled her, and she knew it. Papa hadn't wanted to send her away to finishing school. Mama had demanded it. And while Papa doted upon Addy, it was Mama who ruled him.

"I'm still high-spirited," Addy said. "Nothing has changed."

"Much to your mother's dismay," Aunt Pearl said fondly. "Although I must say, you know I have boundless tolerance for your adventures, dear."

Ah, here was the reprimand Addy had been awaiting.

She winced. "Of course you do, and that is why you are my favorite aunt."

"I'm also your only aunt," Aunt Pearl shrewdly pointed

out with raised brows. "I do find it rather poor that you lied to us all."

"I prefer to think of it as a necessity rather than a lie," Addie hedged. "If Mama or Papa or you had known that I was surprising Lila and Letty with my visit, I have no doubt they would have opposed the trip."

"Hmm," Aunt Pearl said, compressing her lips and regarding Addy in the way she had when Addy had been a naughty child who had played yet another trick upon someone in the household.

"What was I to have done?" Addie asked. "The duke refuses to allow Lila and Letty to visit me in New York City. I had no choice but to come to them."

"But you *didn't* come to them, my dear." Aunt Pearl shook her head, looking august, tender, and disapproving all at once in the way that only she truly could. "They're not even in residence."

Addie huffed out a breath. "And believe me, I never would have come here if I had known that. Why, it's soon Christmas, and now we're to be stranded in the snow with the Duke of Arse-ingham."

Aunt Pearl issued a long-suffering sigh. "You really ought not to call him that, my dear."

"He'll never know."

Dandy chose that moment to leap from Addy's lap and have a bout of animated running about the chamber. Her paws flew across the threadbare Axminster, taking her toward the closed door.

"Dandy, no," Addy called.

But Dandy ignored her as usual, sliding into the door and then scrambling about to race the length of the room a second time before running back to the door again. Dandy tended to have random bursts, and it was best to simply let her run until she collapsed on her side, her mouth hanging slack and her tongue lolling.

"I do think His Grace may discover her presence in your room sooner or later," Aunt Pearl observed.

Addy crossed her arms over her chest. "Let him find her, then. I won't allow him to send her to the stables. She's too delicate for that. She requires warmth and love and baths."

As if to prove Addy's point, Dandy returned to the fireplace and lay on her side, her stomach toward the heat of the flames.

Aunt Pearl sighed. "Oh, my dear girl. I have a feeling you and the duke are going to be at daggers drawn."

Addy glanced down at Dandy, thinking the little brindle French bulldog quite the most lovable dog in all the world. Far more lovable than the Duke of Marchingham could ever dream of being.

"We already are."

THERE WAS, quite suddenly, a great bit of commotion in the room above Lion's study. Thumps and a scrambling sound followed by a *thwack*, then more rhythmic bumps. He cocked his head toward the tumult, listening. It sounded almost as if someone were racing about the chamber.

He frowned at the report from his steward that he had been halfheartedly perusing.

Was someone *running* upstairs?

The notion was preposterous. And yet, as he listened, there was no denying what he was hearing. But who would do such an unseemly thing?

The moment the question occurred to him, Lion had his answer.

Miss Adelia Fox. No one else would be so daring, so outrageous, so insufferably uncouth.

He settled his pen in his inkwell and stood. Was the woman mad? Why would she be running about her bedroom and slamming into doors? Had she not already tortured him enough with her unexpected presence here at Marchingham Hall? Now she was rendering it altogether impossible for him to concentrate.

Lion stalked to the window, where the park beyond was blanketed in white and the snowflakes falling from the sky showed no sign of slowing. If this kept up, the roads would remain impassable for days. Perhaps even a week or—sweet God above—more. He was as stuck with the dreadful Miss Fox as her carriage was mired in the snowbank.

Irritated at the very thought of sharing the same roof with the vexing American, he quit his study, determined to confront her. He was halfway up the staircase before it occurred to him that it wasn't done for a gentleman to knock at the door of an unwed woman, even if she decidedly wasn't a lady.

Lion paused. He could ring for Mrs. Burton or perhaps even one of the few maids left belowstairs. Any one of them might do, and without the danger to Miss Fox's dubious reputation. His fingers tightened on the railing. No, he couldn't rely on any other female in his household. He had no doubt that Miss Fox would simply browbeat them into accepting her eccentric whims.

It would have to be Lion.

With each footfall that took him closer to the room she'd been given, his annoyance grew. She had already interrupted his solitude. She had appeared uninvited. She had brought a *dog* as a companion. She had nearly managed to freeze to death in a broken-down carriage. And now, she was disturbing his peace.

Disregarding the tranquility of his household.

He had no doubt Marchingham Hall was a paltry comparison to her father's magnificent mansion in New York City. However, it was his ancestral home, and she was a guest, albeit an unwanted one. Lion reached her door and raised his fist to rap on it. The very least she could do was to—

The door opened, and the maiden aunt who had also accompanied Miss Adelia Fox, Miss Pearl Fox, gave a start as she nearly collided with him.

"Your Grace!" she squeaked.

He rolled his lips inward and offered a slight bow. "Miss Fox."

"Forgive me my lack of grace," the elder Miss Fox said. "I didn't intend to trample you."

She was a handsome woman, with a pleasant, soft-cheeked visage, gold spectacles perched on her nose, and kindly blue eyes, her ebony curls shot through with silver. She was dressed elegantly in an austere travel gown, and he very much doubted that she had been the one racing about in the chamber.

His eyes narrowed. "It is I who must beg your pardon, Miss Fox. I heard a disturbance and came to investigate the source."

"A disturbance?" The elder Miss Fox blinked owlishly. "Oh, that must have been me. Do forgive me."

"You," he repeated, disbelief tingeing his voice.

"Yes, it was me. I saw a mouse, you see."

Something that sounded suspiciously like a bark emerged from deeper within the room. Lion was a head taller than Miss Fox, and although he'd been trying to avert his gaze in a gentlemanly fashion, he looked up and spied Miss Adelia Fox by the fireplace, wrapped in a blanket, her feet shockingly bare as they were propped up by the fire, her golden hair unbound and cascading down her back...and was that a mongrel stretched on the carpets?

The elder Miss Fox jostled into him and snapped the door closed at her back.

"I was just off to dress for dinner, Your Grace," Miss Fox said.

And that was when Lion realized that Miss Adelia Fox was not alone in being a menace. Apparently, *all* the Misses Fox were lying, shameless bits of baggage. Even the one old enough to be his mother.

"Is the hound within?" he asked tightly.

The elder Miss Fox blinked yet again. "That would have been the mice."

"Mice do not bark, Miss Fox."

"Perhaps my niece sneezed," she suggested brightly. "If you'll excuse me, Your Grace?"

Without awaiting his response, she hastened down the hall and disappeared into the room she'd been allotted. Lion turned back to the closed door before him, the acute sensation of losing control of his own damned household making his gut clench.

To the devil with propriety. Who was here to witness his ungentlemanly behavior? He had naught but a handful of domestics. Snow had blanketed the world. And Miss Adelia Fox had defied him.

He rapped sharply on her door.

On *his* door, as it happened.

"Yes?"

Her dulcet voice was distant, as if she were still by the fire. Unbidden, the image of her rose in his mind. She had removed her stockings. He'd witnessed the curve of a shapely calf, a slim ankle. Heat prickled over his skin, awareness seeping through him. Had her gown been raised any higher, he might have seen her knees.

What was wrong with him? He had no wish to see Miss Adelia Fox's knees.

Did he?

Lion cleared his throat.

"It's Marchingham," he said. "I am desirous of a word with you, madam."

"Well, I am not desirous of a word with you, my lord," she called.

He set his teeth on edge. "I am not a lord, Miss Fox. I am a duke."

"In America, we don't have such silly customs. You'll have to forgive me for my confusion. I'm an uncivilized Yankee."

Fury rose within him. He was being insulted by a bloody door. The maddening woman hadn't even deigned to open it.

"Is refusing to open a door to the person speaking to you also a product of being an uncivilized Yankee?" he snapped.

Muffled footsteps sounded within, and in the next breath, the portal opened just wide enough to reveal one green eye and the corner of her lush pink lips. "What do you want, Marchingham?"

Lion clenched his jaw so hard that the muscles ached. "I want to know why the mongrel isn't in the stables."

"I don't know what you're talking about."

Proving her a liar, the hound's face appeared near the floor, or rather a black nose and a wrinkly forehead, accompanied by loud, pronounced sniffing.

He raised a brow. "I'm talking about the dog at your feet."

"Oh, Dandy is not a dog."

"Surely you aren't going to insult my intelligence by suggesting it's a mouse," he drawled.

Had the snow ceased yet? He certainly hoped it had. Why couldn't the vexing chit have decided to invite herself in summer instead? He'd have already had her waiting for the next train out of here by now.

"Of course not," Miss Fox said brightly. "I would never dream of insulting your intelligence, Your Graceship."

His gaze narrowed. "The correct form of address is *Your Grace*, Miss Fox."

She beamed. "As I said."

"No, you didn't."

"Yes, I did."

"No, you—" Lion stopped himself, gritting his teeth. Why was he arguing with this lunatic? "Explain, if you please. If the snuffling thing at your feet isn't a dog, then what, precisely, is it?"

He could hardly wait for her response.

"She is my darling," Miss Fox answered. "My baby. I am her mama, you see."

"You cannot be a mother to a mongrel."

Miss Fox sighed, shaking her head. "I'm afraid you're wrong, my lord."

She was mocking him. Intentionally addressing him incorrectly.

"Also, Dandelion is *not* a mongrel," she added. "She hails from exquisite French bulldog bloodlines in Paris."

As if to concur, the hound barked at him. Then barked again. And again.

She was irritatingly loud for such a small dog.

Lion winced. "I told you to take it to the stables where it belongs."

"You'll have to take me to the stables as well," Miss Fox announced over the incessant barking.

In the next moment, the dog wedged herself through the door and raced off down the hall.

"Dandy!" Miss Fox called after her.

The dog, quite predictably, didn't listen. Instead, Dandelion rushed down the staircase.

"Oh, bother," Miss Fox muttered.

He couldn't deny it. Watching the mongrel's flagrant refusal to heed Miss Fox pleased him immeasurably.

"It seems your hound obeys as well as you do, madam," he couldn't help but gloat.

"I don't obey, sir."

With a huff, Miss Fox whisked past him, treating him to another tantalizing glimpse of her bare ankles and toes. Lion watched her rush off after the errant French bulldog and tamped down an unwanted rush of appreciation.

*Mayhem.*

That was what this was.

The sooner Miss Adelia Fox and her furred nuisance were gone from Marchingham Hall, the better.

# CHAPTER 3

The dinner table was quiet, save for the clinking of cutlery on plates that had seen more than their fair share of wear. Mama would have been appalled to see her table laid with crockery so well-used. Marchingham didn't seem particularly ashamed of the plates or the plain fare offered for their meal.

But then, he hadn't been expecting guests.

From his aloof silence, Addy suspected he didn't often entertain. Or if he did, he was appallingly bad at it. She supposed either could have been possible.

But as the disapproving quiet stretched on, she found she could no longer hold her tongue, even if Aunt Pearl was doing her utmost to enjoy her meal. Alfred had taken his dinner belowstairs, leaving just the two of them to suffer the duke's icy presence.

"I've yet to see a Christmas tree here at Marchingham Hall," she blurted.

Marchingham paused in the act of cutting a piece of meat, his glacial stare lifting to her. "That is because there isn't one."

She gasped. "No Christmas tree? At home, my mother has the servants erect the tree at least three weeks in advance."

With Christmas a mere fortnight away, it had rather shocked Addy to discover nary a hint of anything festive to be found on her cursory exploration of the manor house. Dandy had led her on quite a merry chase through the halls and rooms. But there had been no kissing boughs, no mistletoe, no fir branches, no candles or trees or ornaments. The entire edifice was bereft.

"As you can see, you are not at home, Miss Fox," he pointed out, his tone cutting.

The urge to fling a forkful of bland roast at his handsome face was strong. But summoning all of her restraint, Addy controlled herself.

She pinned a false smile to her lips. "That's as obvious as the nose on your face."

One golden brow rose, his countenance forbidding. "Are you commenting upon the size of my nose, madam?"

Aunt Pearl made a strangled sound at Addy's side, and Addy cast a glance in her direction to make certain she wasn't choking on her food. Aunt Pearl hastily took a sip of her wine, giving Addy a meaningful look.

Her aunt wished for Addy to hold her tongue, she knew. But there was something about the wretched duke and the misery of her present circumstances that brought out the very worst in her. As the snow exhibited no sign of slowing, she was stuck with him, all whilst her dear friends were nowhere near. At least after she had located Dandy, she had slipped the French bulldog back into her room without Marchingham taking note.

The victory was Addy's sole source of comfort at present.

She flicked a glance back in the duke's direction, thinking it a pity that such uncommonly fine looks had been gifted upon a man who was as pleasant as a cold, wet stocking.

"I would never dream of commenting upon the size of your nose, Your Graceship," she said, unable to keep from needling him just a bit by once again intentionally using the incorrect form of address.

His nostrils flared and his lips compressed. "Yes, I reckon to do so would be unbearably rude, and you would never be that, would you, Miss Fox?"

She narrowed her eyes at him, reconsidering her decision not to throw food at his head from across the table. "Never."

They exchanged glares, and then the duke resumed eating his dinner.

Addy waited for him to take a bite before continuing brightly, "If you don't have a Christmas tree, then we must find you one."

He took his time chewing and swallowing before responding simply, "No."

"No? That is all you have to say on the matter?"

A small smile curved the corners of his mouth upward. "Quite."

Her fingers clenched on her own fork, her grip so tight that her knuckles ached. "At home in New York City, we have a beautiful tree covered in ornaments and candles, festoons over every doorway, kissing balls, presents, candy canes… It is a truly glorious sight to behold. No one celebrates Christmas like my mama. That is why I wanted Lila and Letty to join us."

"No good would have come of my sisters visiting you in America, Miss Fox," he said calmly.

"What would have been the harm?" she demanded, still outraged by his refusals each year.

"You, Miss Fox. I daresay your influence is hardly improving."

"*Me?*" Her shoulders went back. "There is nothing wrong with my influence."

He regarded her solemnly. "What would you call sewing the undergarments of the headmistress together whilst she was sleeping?"

"Hilarious," she said, raising her wineglass in mock toast. "Madame Mallette was horrid to us. She deserved far worse than having the split in her drawers sewn shut. Although, I will admit I was delighted to know that she failed to realize what we had done until she had gone to the water closet and it was too late."

"Addy, dearest," Aunt Pearl attempted to intervene in a tone of shock.

Addy knew it was beyond the pale to speak so boldly in mixed company, but she didn't care.

"Is a pot of honey emptied in one's hair a worse fate?" he inquired coldly.

"The honey wasn't my idea," she defended herself. "However, it was immensely gratifying to see how difficult of a time that old shrew had washing it out."

"What about sneaking into the village to find young gentlemen to kiss?" he snapped.

Heat crept up Addy's throat, but she refused to look away. Instead, she held his gaze. "That one *was* my idea."

It had also been what had ultimately seen Addy, Lila, and Letty expelled from the Académie Clairemont.

"Adelia Louise," Aunt Pearl said, sounding aghast.

Mama had never told anyone the true reason for Addy's premature return from Swiss finishing school. She'd been far too ashamed. Poor Aunt Pearl was learning of Addy's misadventures for the first time. All thanks to the Duke of Arseingham.

"As you can see, I was not unreasonably reluctant to allow my sisters to once more be exposed to your unladylike influence," the duke was saying with a self-important, triumphant air. "They might have gone to visit you and ended up murdered in some filthy alley or perhaps they would have run off with a pair of lowly sailors."

"I never would have allowed any harm to befall them," she defended herself, fairly trembling with outrage. "Lila and Letty are like sisters to me."

"You must forgive me if I find your reassurances less than comforting, Miss Fox," he returned, his voice cool. "It is a miracle neither of them was ruined after what happened at the Académie Clairemont, and all thanks to you."

A thought suddenly occurred to her, distracting her from the acerbic dialogue she was exchanging with the duke. The Christmas presents she had painstakingly chosen and brought from America for Letty and Lila were packed in her trunks. The trunks she'd been forced to abandon hours earlier to the snow.

She gasped. "I have to go back to the carriage."

"So that you can meet your worldly end in the snowbank after all?" Marchingham asked unkindly.

"No." Tears welled in her eyes. Tears of frustration and sadness and failure. Oh, how she had been looking forward to seeing Lila and Letty again at last. To presenting them with their gifts. To staying up far too late, exchanging stories about the turns their lives had taken over the last three years. "So that I can rescue the presents I brought for your sisters from the snow."

On the last word, her voice cracked. She very much didn't want to exhibit any weakness to the duke. Particularly not after his harsh words and stinging accusations. But much to her humiliation, the tears spilled, rolling hot and fast down her cheeks.

Christmas was ruined. She hadn't managed to surprise her friends. She was trapped with their horrible brother. It was still snowing. And she had no clothing, aside from the travel gown on her back.

"Don't cry, Adelia dear," Aunt Pearl said softly, patting her hand. "You'll make me weep too."

Addy sniffled. Swallowed. Dashed at the tears with the back of her hand. How embarrassing. She was Miss Adelia Fox, daughter of one of the wealthiest men in New York City, and yet she had never felt more helpless, nor more like a failure.

"You needn't weep, Miss Fox," the duke said curtly.

His words—far less cold than his earlier tone—caught her attention. She'd supposed he would triumph over her sadness, her inability to control her own emotions. But there was, unless she was mistaken, a hint of sympathy in his voice now, in his gaze as it met hers and held.

"Your trunks have all been collected," he said gruffly.

Addy's mouth fell open. "They have?"

He nodded. "A few of the lads and I returned to the carriage, and we loaded them into a wagon and brought them here."

He had exhibited such callous indifference over her concerns earlier. And yet, he had ventured into the snow yet again on her behalf. Addy didn't quite know what to do with this information.

"Thank you," she told him, unable to keep the astonishment from her voice.

He returned his attention to his plate. "The grooms were brushing the snow from them in the stables. I expect you'll find them awaiting you in your room after dinner."

"I am indebted to you," Addy managed, though the admission was not without another wound to her already fragile pride.

"Indeed you are, Miss Fox," he agreed, his eyes lifting from his plate to hers once again.

She swallowed, not liking being beholden to him or the way she couldn't help but to admire how very handsome he looked, the lamplight glinting in his golden hair. He had dressed formally this evening, in a black coat and trousers, a gray damask waistcoat, and a crisp white neckcloth. He would have looked at home in any of the social gatherings in New York City in his elegant attire, and yet she knew instinctively he would have stood out. When he almost smiled, he was nothing short of beautiful, and much to her dismay, she found herself wondering what it would feel like to have that harsh, unforgiving mouth on hers.

When he raised an imperious brow at her again, Addy realized that she was staring at him. Having improper thoughts she ought never to have about a man as cold and unfeeling as the Duke of Marchingham. She reached for her wine and took a bracing sip, aware of the furious heat creeping up her neck and reaching her cheeks.

What was wrong with her? The man had orchestrated the rescue of her trunks and her person, but that was all. She didn't like him, and it didn't matter how lovely he was to behold.

An awkward silence descended once more, and Addy turned her attention firmly to the consumption of her roast and *haricot verts*, which had turned cold.

"That was most kind of you to fetch dear Addy's trunks," Aunt Pearl ventured. "You have been a godsend to us all."

Addy stifled the urge to kick her aunt beneath the table. The man was already insufferable. There was no need to further inflate his opinion of himself.

"Despite the unexpected nature of your visit, I aim to be an affable host," he said mildly.

Addy snorted. An affable host might have avoided pointing out that they were uninvited guests.

"Did you say something, Miss Fox?" he asked.

"Nothing at all, Your Grace," she answered with mock sweetness.

Addy swore the corners of his mouth twitched, as if he suppressed a smile. But his countenance remained implacable as he returned to his meal in more silence.

Lion slowly pulled himself from the depths of slumber to the realization that someone—or perhaps more accurately some*thing*—was licking his face. His eyes jolted open, and in the low light of the flickering hearth, he discovered a dark, furred beast perched on his chest. Said beast moved enthusiastically to his ear, licking behind it.

"Good God," he grumbled, knowing at once what the thing was.

Dandy.

The French bulldog that had been destroying the solitude of his home ever since she had arrived shivering and wrapped in a blanket, held in the elder Miss Fox's arms as if she were a baby. It had taken remarkably little time to prove that she was not, in fact, an innocent babe, but instead the spawn of Beelzebub.

"Cease that at once," he snapped.

Dandy didn't even pause in her ministrations. Instead, he felt the sharp prick of teeth on his earlobe as the dog took a nibble.

"Damnation." He lifted the squirming dog from his chest. "Bad Dandy."

Lion settled her on the floor and sat up, wincing at a twinge in his back as he rubbed his ear. He had been reading in the library, too unsettled to sleep, some port at hand, and his eyes had grown heavy. Instead of venturing to his bedchamber, he had lain on the Grecian couch with the intention of closing his eyes for a few moments.

Given the darkness beyond the windows, it looked as if he had slept for far longer than he'd intended.

Dandy leapt onto the cushion and rose on her hind legs to lick his ear again.

"Curse it, mongrel," he growled, rising to his feet to glower down at the boisterous dog. "Why aren't you in the stables where you belong?"

He had his answer when a familiar voice called quietly from beyond the library.

"Dandy? Where are you, my naughty little darling?"

Lovely. Now he was going to have to face Miss Fox. *Alone.* In the shadows of the night.

"Dandy?" she called again.

The dog's pointed ears went up, and she angled her face toward the partially ajar door, listening. Then she jumped from the couch and raced across the carpets.

Lion had but a moment to compose himself, running a hand through his hair in an effort to tame the wayward waves that were a constant source of irritation to him, before Miss Fox appeared in the doorway.

Wearing nothing but a nightgown.

His mouth went dry and desire unfurled within him, like a summer rose suddenly blooming. Her hair was unbound, falling down her back as it had been when he had spied her sitting before the fire earlier. Once again, her toes were bare beneath the hem of her gown. As she moved, the fabric clung to her decadent feminine form in all the best places, making him uncomfortably aware that she was not wearing a corset. Her breasts were round and full and tempting, her waist and hips deliciously curved.

"There you are," she said, bending down to pat Dandy on the head, clearly unaware of his presence in the shadows. "It wouldn't do for the dreadful duke to realize you've been running about."

The dreadful duke?

Grimly, Lion cleared his throat.

Miss Fox jumped and straightened, emitting a high-pitched squeal. "Marchingham. I didn't know you were there."

He moved toward her. "That much is woefully apparent."

As was the fact that her nipples were now hard. Rude, pointed tips jutting toward him. A temptation he should not be noticing. This was Miss Adelia Fox, scandalous hoyden and menace to his sanity and his sisters' reputations. The proof was before him. No lady would leave her bedchamber in the midst of the night in such a shocking state of dishabille, particularly when she was staying in someone else's home.

She was a problem. *Trouble.* Just like her ear-eating dog.

"I hope you weren't eavesdropping on my private conversation with Dandy," she said with the airs of a queen.

Miss Adelia Louise Fox was the most outlandish woman he had ever met.

"Did you just smile?" she asked, suspicion in her voice.

Was he smiling? Good God, he actually *was*. How utterly horrifying.

Lion stopped before her, which was a mistake because the proximity made her scent rush over him, violets and orris root and soft, warm woman. For a mindless moment, he found himself wondering if her perfume would linger in his bedclothes and upon his pillow. But then he realized how ludicrous such a thought was, and he promptly banished it.

"I cannot help my natural reaction to preposterous behavior, Miss Fox," he told her.

She eyed him curiously as the little dog sat upon her feet, facing him as well with dark-brown eyes. "You aren't angry?"

"Angry that your dog decided to make a meal of my ear whilst I was asleep? Angry that she isn't in the stables where she belongs? Or angry that you insulted me to the hound in question?"

Her lips parted.

He wished she weren't so bloody beautiful.

"Have I rendered you speechless, Miss Fox?" he pressed, rather enjoying himself.

He had no doubt that she wasn't ordinarily silent. The woman was bold and opinionated and brazen.

"I'm never speechless," she countered, apparently having found her tongue. "What did you mean when you said Dandy made a meal of your ear?"

"I felt teeth."

She nibbled her lower lip, drawing Lion's attention to the sensual allure of her mouth. "She adores ears. She'd never truly bite them hard enough to cause harm. But sometimes she's enthusiastic and forgets herself."

The dog was as ill-mannered as Miss Fox was.

For some reason, Lion didn't say that thought aloud.

"What are you doing wandering about in the midst of the night?" he inquired instead. "Surely you realize it isn't done to leave your chamber without at least a dressing gown."

He would not look at her nipples. He would not look at her nipples. He would not—

His gaze fell to where the puckered buds continued to protrude in an erotic taunt from beneath the fine fabric of her nightgown. His cock twitched. What was wrong with him? Lion forced his stare back to her face where it belonged.

"Dandy was scratching at the door," Miss Fox explained. "She needed to venture out of doors for a moment. But after we came back inside from the garden, she had one of her happy bouts and raced away, and I couldn't find her. She must have run into the library and discovered you there."

Lion was reasonably certain the woman was as mad as a Bedlamite.

"A happy bout? Good God, what is that?"

"It's when she suddenly tears off on a joyful sprint," Miss Fox explained. "There's no telling where she'll go or when it will end."

And the mongrel was equally insane.

"I've never heard of a dog doing something so illogical."

Miss Fox beamed. "Well, now you have. Dandy doesn't give a fig about logic. Do you know why, Your Grace? Because she's a dog. Her primary concerns are being loved, being warm, and not allowing anyone near her favorite blanket or her bowl of food."

Her incessant cheer vexed him. Why was she always smiling? Why did she speak to him as if he were a small child incapable of understanding complex thought?

"You should go back to bed, Miss Fox," he told her.

But damn him if uttering the word *bed* in reference to his unwanted houseguest didn't cause his stupid cock to harden. It was her scent. Her nearness. All that glorious hair tumbling down her back. The exquisite fullness of her breasts.

Those nipples.

His breath was tight in his chest. It had been a long time since Lion had allowed himself to be tempted by a woman. Since he'd permitted himself to feel the slightest stirrings of attraction.

She cocked her head, considering him. "Why are you not abed at this hour? Why were you sleeping in the library?"

He wasn't going to admit it was because her presence had caused him so much upheaval that he hadn't been able to sleep. That he had ventured to the library to read and sip port until he had finally, mercifully passed out.

"Because this is my home, and I can do whatever I wish in

it, whenever I choose to do so," he snapped, annoyed with the fire in his blood, all caused by her.

She was unsuitable. Far from a lady. Appallingly mannerless. He disliked her. Quite strongly. This mad awareness of her was base lust, and he could control himself. He was a gentleman above all else.

But then she smiled serenely, and when Miss Adelia Fox smiled, she was nothing short of gorgeous.

"Of course this is your home," she said agreeably. "You may sleep wherever you like. Perhaps in the stables, even."

She was mocking him, the daring minx.

He clenched his jaw. "You are astonishingly brazen, madam."

"I've been told so on more than one occasion."

He didn't doubt that.

"The lack of contrition in your voice suggests you don't care."

She winked and leaned toward him as if she were imparting a delicate secret. "You are correct, Your Graceship."

She smelled so alluring. And her green eyes were dancing with amusement. He didn't know which he wanted to do more—argue with Miss Fox, or kiss her.

Neither was the best course of action, naturally.

"Your Grace," he corrected coolly instead, though he was fairly certain that Miss Fox was more than aware that her form of address was wrong.

She bent and scooped the seated dog into her arms while Lion made every effort to avoid looking at her luscious breasts swaying beneath her nightgown. Dandy licked her cheek adoringly.

"That is what I said," she informed him without a hint of humility. "Now, if you will excuse us, I fear all this travel has made me quite exhausted. Dandy and I must return to our room."

She was dismissing him? And carrying away that blasted dog to once more roost in one of his beds?

"Dogs don't roost, Your Graceship," the hoyden called over her shoulder. "They aren't chickens, you know."

Christ, had he spoken aloud? Lion watched her leave the library, the subtle movement of her hips mesmerizing him as he rubbed his jaw.

"Your Graceship," he muttered to himself.

It damned well better stop snowing by the morning.

THE NEXT MORNING, Addy was sneaking from the breakfast room bearing a napkin laden with bacon, kippers, and a poached egg for Dandy when a frigid voice stayed her.

"Is there a reason you are carrying a sack of food away from the breakfast room, Miss Fox?"

With a sigh, she stopped and spun about to find the Duke of Marchingham looming, dressed this morning in tweed and looking like the epitome of a handsome English country gentleman, quite as if he had stepped out of the pages of a monthly fashion publication. Pity his exceptional looks and form were wasted upon such a wretched man.

She held the napkin behind her back and forced her brightest smile. "Good morning to you as well, Your Grace. I'm afraid you must be mistaken. I haven't a sack of food at all."

"A *makeshift* sack, then," he corrected, enunciating his words in a way that made them sound like a caress, "composed of a napkin stuffed with kippers and a poached egg."

Well, drat. Apparently, the duke had been somehow watching her without her notice. She had taken great care.

The dining room had been empty, save herself and Aunt Pearl, whom she had left behind to finish her own breakfast.

Her chin went up, and she held his stare with a challenge of her own. "You forgot the bacon."

"You might have better enjoyed your spoils at the table. I didn't realize it was an American custom to drag table scraps away like a wild dog."

Had she thought him wretched? The word seemed far too tame. The Duke of Marchingham was positively vile. But she was determined to meet his forbidding ice with the sunniest of dispositions.

Addy forced a smile. "Yes, it is indeed an American custom. We also enjoy taking leisurely strolls in thunderstorms and wearing our drawers on our heads instead of hats."

Ruddy color flared on his high cheekbones. "Charming little eccentricities, to be sure. Tell me, do you ordinarily feed your hound from the breakfast table?"

"No, of course not. I have a special meal prepared for her." The napkin was yet held like a guilty secret behind her back, even though Marchingham was more than aware of its presence and what she intended to do with it.

"What manner of special meal?"

Was it her imagination, or had his wintry gaze dipped for a moment to her bodice?

No, she didn't think it was. Addy thought of how his eyes had traveled over her last evening in the library. She'd been all too aware of the thin layer of silk covering her. But surely the Duke of Marchingham wasn't attracted to her. He had made his disdain for her abundantly clear.

She eyed him curiously, wondering if the color had deepened. "Forgive me if I find your concern for the dishes I serve Dandy somewhat odd, given your determination to see her banished to your stables."

"If it means keeping you from thieving the napkins from the dining room, then perhaps I ought to accommodate you."

"I'm not thieving it," she denied, insulted. "I would have returned it when Dandy was finished."

"I'm half persuaded the little beggar would have eaten the napkin as well," he drawled. "You have leave to request whatever you require for the hound during your brief stay here."

She noted his emphasis on the word *brief* in regard to her visit to Marchingham Hall and couldn't quite tamp down the surge of irritation. The snow was falling with considerably less vigor this morning, a sure indication the massive storm was at last moving on. But that didn't change the fact that she was likely going to be stranded here as an unwanted guest for the next few days at least, if not longer.

Which also meant she would be perilously close to enduring Christmas with Letty and Lila's terrible brother. Surely the snow would melt sufficiently in less than two weeks, however. At least, she hoped it would.

"Do you have any notion of when the roads will be passable again?" she asked him, hoping he might have an answer.

But the duke shook his head and clasped his hands behind his back. "Sadly, no. After the snow finally ceases falling, I may have a better idea. However, much depends upon the temperatures. If this cold persists, it's doubtful that the snow will begin to melt in the next few days. It could take a week or longer."

"Oh." Despite her determination to maintain an unaffected mien of bright, ceaseless cheer, Addy couldn't keep the disappointment from her voice.

This would be her first Christmas without Mama and Papa, and she wouldn't even have the company of her dear friends to help distract her from missing them. Because although Letty and Lila were a day's train ride away, if the snow on the roads didn't sufficiently melt, there was no way she would be able to reach them in time for Christmas.

"I will be every bit as relieved when the snow begins melting as you, Miss Fox," he said coldly. "Now, please do arrange for your mongrel to receive a proper meal and do whatever you must with the bundle you're holding behind your back."

Addy struggled to maintain her smile as she brought the napkin to the front of her body, dangling it in the air at her waist. The cloth was already beginning to darken from bacon grease. And whilst Dandy adored bacon, sometimes the richness of the treat didn't agree with her delicate constitution. Addy had been hesitant to settle upon the bacon, but she'd been faced with few possibilities. Now, the duke had grudgingly offered to allow her to request a proper meal for her dog.

"Is there any chance you've yet to break your fast?" she asked wryly, extending the napkin bundle in the duke's direction.

He eyed it dubiously. "I have. I wake at dawn."

Silence stretched between them for a few moments, and Addy found herself strangely at a loss for words. His icy gaze held her in its relentless thrall, captivating her. She lowered the napkin awkwardly, still uncertain of what she ought to do with it.

"Dawn," she repeated at last. "It's half past ten now."

He raised a brow. "Indeed."

"Did you sleep in your library all night?" she asked then, curious.

"Where I slept is none of your concern, madam."

Of course it wasn't. And when he phrased it thus, his words held an inherent intimacy.

"I'm sorry that Dandy woke you," she said, feeling heat creep up her own throat.

"See that you maintain control of her when she has her happy bouts, won't you? If she is set upon running about my home, causing a disturbance, it will be out to the stables with her after all."

"Do you harbor a strident dislike for dogs, or are you always this autocratic?" she asked before she could think better of her words. "Letty and Lila warned me, but it seems I didn't take sufficient heed."

His shoulders stiffened. "What did they say about me?"

It occurred to her that she could be miring her friends in trouble with their disapproving brother. And as far as the Duke of Marchingham was concerned, Addy had already done that once in the past, to disastrous consequences.

"Only that you are very firm in your edicts," she hastened to say. "And proper."

A muscle in his jaw clenched. "One must be firm, particularly when it concerns wayward young ladies who are easily led astray."

It was a veiled reference to their days at the Académie Clairemont.

"Letty and Lila are not easily led astray," she defended her friends. "It was hardly our fault that finishing school was so deadly dull."

"And you had nothing better to do than lead my innocent sisters on an expedition to ruination?" he asked sharply.

So sharply that Addy cast a glance in the direction of the dining room door, wondering if Aunt Pearl could hear their squabbles.

"It was hardly an expedition to ruination," she countered, her smile at last faltering.

One would have to possess the patience of a saint to contend with the Duke of Marchingham and maintain good cheer. The man was an ominous thundercloud on an otherwise faultless summer day.

He closed the polite distance that had existed between them, towering over her. His shoulders were even broader than she had recalled from last night in the shadows when he had been in nothing more than his shirt sleeves. How annoyingly handsome he had looked then, his hair ruffled and his customary icy mask less severe from slumber.

"Tell me, Miss Fox," he said, his voice low and deceptively pleasant, floating over her like steam from a hot bath. "How many village lads did you kiss that day before Madame Mallette found you?"

None, but she wasn't about to admit that to him. The three of them hadn't even found any obliging lads. They had managed to obtain some wine at a tavern before Madame had stormed in, furious to find the three of them giggling at a scarred old table.

Their adventures had been promptly at an end.

"Half a dozen or so," she lied. "Some of them were more proficient than others. If only Madame hadn't found us so soon. Perhaps I could have kissed even more."

The red returned to the duke's cheekbones, and his nostrils flared.

"Your father ought to have taken a reed to your backside when you returned to America," he said.

"Your Graceship," she mocked lightly. "I am astonished that you are thinking about my backside."

The color deepened.

His gaze dipped to her mouth, just for a fleeting moment, and she wondered what he was thinking. Was he imagining her kissing those nonexistent Swiss men? Was he repulsed by her, or was he thinking about what it would be like to kiss her himself?

His head bent toward hers. Her heart beat faster, warmth pooling deep within her. She swayed toward him ever so slightly, tempted to feel those forbidding lips on hers.

"Do take the napkin of scraps to the kitchens, Miss Fox," he snapped, straightening to his full, impressive height again. "Cook will attend to it, and I'm sure she'll be more than happy to provide you with whatever you require for the hound."

With a formal bow, he stalked past her, leaving Addy to watch his purposeful strides take him down the hall, where he disappeared into a room and closed the door with more purpose than required. He slammed it, in fact.

*Well.*

Perhaps Addy had managed to get beneath the Duke of Arse-ingham's impeccable skin.

It was only then that she realized she hadn't an inkling of where the kitchens to the sprawling manor house were. She sighed. Time to find Mrs. Burton or one of the chambermaids and inquire after its placement.

Aunt Pearl ventured from the dining room in a swish of skirts, looking far more regal in her navy day gown now that their trunks had been restored to them and they had each been granted the aid of a maid for dressing. She cast a meaningful look in Addy's direction.

"Do you think it wise to continue to prod the duke, my dear girl?" she asked shrewdly.

Addy wondered just how much her aunt had overheard. Renewed warmth stung her cheeks, but she refused to acknowledge it.

She wasn't ashamed of her boldness.

"Wise? Of course not." She paused and sent her aunt a cheeky wink. "But it certainly is amusing."

Aunt Pearl sighed, shaking her head. "Adelia Louise, I have no notion of what goes through that wild mind of yours."

"Neither do I sometimes," Addy admitted quietly, casting another look in the direction of Marchingham's closed door.

She had never met a gentleman she wanted to simultaneously punch and kiss before. It was certainly a novel discovery. Pity she could do neither in this instance. He was their host and Letty and Lila's elder brother. Neither kissing him nor blackening his eye would be wise.

"Let's find someone to help steer us to the kitchens, then," Aunt Pearl said with a resigned tone, patting her arm. "You'll be wanting to rid yourself of that napkin of food before it begins to drip all over the carpets or—worse—your lovely gown."

The carpets at Marchingham Hall were in need of replacement. Addy's gown, however, was in the finest fashion, a Worth creation fresh from Paris. The snow had somehow failed to damage the silk, thanks to the tight fit of Addy's trunks.

"Excellent plan," she agreed, starting off with her aunt in the opposite direction of the duke. "I'm so glad you agreed to accompany me here instead of Mama. She wouldn't have been nearly as much fun."

Aunt Pearl grinned. "I know, my dear girl. I know."

# CHAPTER 4

*Half a dozen or so.*
 By God.

The minx had kissed half the men in the tiny mountain village outside the Swiss finishing school, and she had dared to look him in the eye with defiance sparkling in her emerald gaze and admit it with nary a hint of shame.

As Lion stewed in his study, Miss Fox's words continued to taunt him.

*I am astonished that you are thinking about my backside*, she had said.

Oh, he was thinking about her backside. And her front as well. His thoughts were bloody well consumed with the minx. What her hair looked like flowing freely over her shoulders. The tight little points of her nipples protruding from her nightgown. The full swells of her breasts. The curve of her hips. Her delicate bare feet.

That mouth of hers, always smiling, uttering mockery and taunts at every turn. What he would give to tame those sultry lips with his. To kiss her until she was breathless, her eyes glazed, and there were no more thoughts of vexing him running wild in her clever brain.

At least the snow had finally stopped.

Lion ran a hand through his hair and paced the length of his study for what must have been the hundredth time that afternoon. He had foregone luncheon to avoid Miss Fox's maddening presence, and now he was hungry and irritable. He ought to have listened to Stevens and taken a tray whilst he finished reviewing the bills that had been sent up from Hawthorne House in London. The efficient running of households and estates was so damned costly, and thanks to the profligate dukes preceding him—his own father included—Lion was left in a constant state of near-destitution.

If only Lila and Violetta would find proper husbands and marry them.

It would be a great deal of weight off his shoulders.

Their father had died when Lion had been a green lad of eighteen, and their mother had gone not long after, leaving Lion to be father and mother to a pair of young girls who had grown to become wayward hellions. They had spent most of their lives in the country, away from London and town bronze. By the time he'd realized how woefully lacking the tutelage of their governess had been, Lila and Violetta had been eighteen and nineteen and had yet to even have their presentations at court.

He had scraped together every last ha'penny to send them to finishing school in an effort to give them the polish and elegance they would need to land suitable matches in polite society.

And then they had been summarily sent home because of the influence of Miss Adelia Fox, a spoiled American hoyden who didn't need sophistication or refinement to recommend her when she had her father's immeasurable fortune. Three years of mounting bills later, and both his sisters still remained unwed.

That was what he needed to remember every time he found himself entranced by Miss Fox's charming retroussé nose or the sparkle in her eyes. She was the source of a great deal of his present state of penury and misery.

She was—

The faint strains of music reached him, causing Lion's strides and his whirling thoughts to both falter. Piano music. Singing.

*Miss Fox.*

He found himself wandering from his study, following the sound to the music room that had been his mother's greatest pride at Marchingham Hall. Lion hadn't played in years, but he kept the instruments tuned for his sisters' sakes.

Neither Lila nor Violetta sang the way Miss Fox did, however.

"See the blazing Yule before us," she crooned.

He stood at the threshold, watching her. Miss Fox's back was to him, her golden hair plaited into an elaborate braid and then woven into a chignon high on her head. Her dainty fingers moved over the ivory keys with ease and skill as she sang.

"Strike the harp and join the chorus," she continued. "Fa la la la la la la la la."

It was a Christmas carol. Of course it was.

He had never seen a woman so dismayed to find a lack of Christmas trees and other maudlin decorations hanging about. And Lion couldn't say why, but he found himself mesmerized by the lilting strains of her husky voice as she reached the final chorus of fa la las.

When she finished, he applauded, and she gave a start at the first clap. Swinging about on the piano bench, she pressed a hand over her heart.

"Oh, Your Grace, you startled me!"

At least she hadn't called him *Your Graceship*, he reasoned, venturing deeper into the music room for unfathomable reasons.

"Forgive me," he said, trying not to take note of the way the sunlight glinted off the snow beyond the window and danced over the burnished gold of her hair. "I heard music, and I couldn't help but to investigate the source."

"Aunt Pearl is weary from our travels as well as yesterday's…well." Miss Fox sent him a wry smile. "As you can imagine, it wasn't our plan for the carriage to become mired in the snowbank, nor for her to have to ride through the snow carrying Dandy. She decided to nap this afternoon with Dandy, and I chose to go exploring. When I discovered the piano, I couldn't resist."

She was rambling, he realized, bemused. Could it be that Miss Adelia Fox, the most brazen and unapologetic woman he had ever met, was embarrassed to have been found commandeering his music room and singing as if she had an audience the size of a cathedral instead of only herself?

Lion stopped just short of the piano bench, near enough to catch the faintest hint of her scent and yet far enough away that he couldn't be tempted to do anything more than observe.

"You are talented at playing and singing, Miss Fox," he said. "Although I may find fault with your choice of song, the melody was delightful."

"You find fault with my choice of song?" she sounded affronted. "What is wrong with 'Deck the Halls,' sir? I think it perfectly agreeable at this time of year."

"This time of year?"

"Christmas, of course." She spoke to him slowly, enunciating as if he were an infant struggling to understand.

At last, *he* was the one who was vexing *her*. Lion was quite enjoying himself.

He shrugged. "I must say, aside from the obligatory visit to the pew, I've never paid much notice to it."

Miss Fox gasped as if he had announced he had recently committed a murder and had been keeping the bloodied knife used to perpetrate the crime hidden beneath his bed.

"Never paid much notice?" she repeated. "Poor Letty and Lila. Little wonder they were desperate to join me in New York City for a Fox family Christmas. Mama hosts a wonderful ball. I would have dearly loved for them to attend. Only the cream of high society is invited, naturally. You needn't have feared that Letty and Lila would have found themselves unacceptable American beaus. Mama is wretchedly haughty when it comes to these sorts of things."

"The ball wasn't the reason I denied them the visit," he said and then could have kicked himself for the way Miss Fox's lovely face instantly fell.

"Ah, yes. How could I forget?" She gave him her customary sunny smile, but it appeared forced. "The reason you wouldn't allow them to come to New York City for Christmas was me."

He held her stare, annoyed with himself for the pang of guilt that went through him at her pronouncement. Why should he feel badly for protecting his sisters? It wasn't as if his concerns were without merit. The hoyden had confessed to kissing half a dozen Swiss lads before Madame Mallette had charged into the tavern and saved Violetta and Lila from certain ruin.

Lion frowned. At least, he hoped they had been saved from ruin. He had never thought to question either of them too deeply on the matter. Questioning one's maiden sisters about kissing made a man deuced uncomfortable. It wasn't proper.

"I'm afraid it was your conduct," he said gently. "I could never, in good conscience, send my sisters away to another continent under the aegis of the hellion who was responsible for their rejection from the Académie Clairemont."

She crossed her arms and huffed indignantly. "Did you come to the music room with the sole intention of insulting me, Your Graceship? If so, you might have just as easily remained hidden away in whatever little ducal dungeon you've been occupying since you stormed away at breakfast."

The sheer daring of this woman.

"I don't have dungeons, ducal or otherwise. And I most certainly wasn't hiding."

Actually, that last bit was a lie. He *had* been hiding. Hiding from her, specifically. But he would sooner choke on the table scraps she'd been carrying away to her mongrel than admit it. Because it was far too damning. The implications… he couldn't even allow himself to turn them over in his mind.

Miss Fox gave him an arch look and then turned back to the piano, settling her fingers over the keys. Without a word, she began to play another song.

"It came upon the midnight clear, that glorious song of old…"

Her voice soared. It moved over him like a caress. Held his rapt attention. He remained, listening. Drinking in the sight and the sound. And he hadn't an inkling why.

*Half a dozen village lads*, he reminded himself bitterly.

But it didn't matter. Because when Adelia Louise Fox sang, it was with a voice to rival the angels. He wanted to bask in it. To capture it somehow so that he could listen to it again and again. Lion knew that he ought to quit the room. That he should return to his study and cease lingering about, listening to her musical efforts.

And yet, he lingered.

When the song was over, she moved on to "The First

Noel" without missing a note, singing it with equal beauty. Despite himself, he was entranced. She was bold and maddening and quite shockingly improper, her lack of manners nothing short of astounding.

But he admired her just the same.

She finished playing and turned back to him, her expression challenging. "You're still here."

He raised an eyebrow and stared her down. "It *is* my music room, Miss Fox."

"I know that, but your disapproval of me hangs over you like a dark storm cloud. I would have thought you'd prefer to be as far from me as possible."

She wasn't wrong about that, but for some reason, Lion felt the sharp prick of guilt at her words.

"I find your singing pleasant," he said stiffly, the only sufficient excuse for remaining here that he could think of.

Her lips parted. "Thank you."

She sounded surprised. Lion found himself mesmerized by her mouth. He wished he could find every one of those half dozen Swiss lads and trounce them for knowing those lips when he didn't.

"You're welcome," he managed, his voice feeling suddenly rusty.

He was hardening in his trousers at the mere thought of kissing her. What the devil was wrong with him? And why couldn't he seem to stop staring at her lips?

"Do you play?" she asked.

"I haven't done so in years," he admitted.

She slid to the side on the piano bench, making room for him. "Come and take a seat, Marchingham. We'll play and sing a song together."

He eyed the space she had created dubiously. "I don't think that would be wise."

"Why not?"

*Because if I'm sitting that near to you, I may be tempted to touch you.*

No, he couldn't very well admit that shocking, horrifying truth now, could he?

Lion cleared his throat. "My skill is abysmal compared to yours."

"Nonsense." She grinned at him.

And God, but it was difficult to keep himself under control when she smiled at him like that, her green eyes sparkling as if they were keeping a secret that only the two of them knew. He could well understand his sisters' affection for her. The woman was a magnetic force even when he desperately wished to be repelled.

"It will be fun," she added. "But then, is that what you're afraid of? That you'll actually enjoy yourself? Good heavens, perhaps you'll even *smile* again."

She was teasing him, the hoyden.

Absurdly, he found himself wanting to return her grin with one of his own.

"I'm not afraid, madam."

She patted the bench. "Then sit."

He felt like a dog, doing his master's bidding.

"I won't bite," she added outrageously. "I promise."

Her words sent a strange rush of heat directly to his groin. Because, curse her, he was thinking about her nibbling on his neck whilst he...

*No. Decidedly not.*

He mustn't allow that dangerous thought to progress any further.

Lion stalked to the bench and seated himself at her side, trying to ignore the scent of violets curling around him.

And failing.

"Do select a song, Miss Fox," he said curtly. "I haven't all day."

※

ADDY COULD SCARCELY SUPPRESS her glee as Marchingham sat beside her on the piano bench. Fortunately, it was a sturdy piece of furniture and large enough to hold the both of them. The Duke of Marchingham was not a small man. As he had folded his frame into the seat, she had been reminded of just how broad his shoulders were and how long his legs. His thigh pressed against her skirts, crowding her as his scent teased her senses. His proximity was a problem.

She knew that much already.

He settled his hands upon the keys, and Addy couldn't help but admire them. They were so very masculine, his fingers long and elegant, one bearing a signet ring, and for a breathless moment, she wondered what those hands would feel like on her skin. Touching her. Caressing her.

Oh, what was wrong with her?

She didn't even *like* this man. Such thoughts were mad aberrations. She had known handsome gentlemen before. This one was no exception. She could remain unaffected. Her heart would return to a normal rhythm.

Addy turned toward him to find him studying her with his unnerving blue gaze. Her heart continued to beat wildly, and her breath caught in her lungs.

"*Cantique de Noël?*" he asked.

And for a moment, she didn't know what he was saying.

Addy blinked, realizing he had spoken French. The song was familiar to her from her days at the Académie Clairemont. He was thinking about the song while she was mooning over his eyes and his hands and trying not to notice how beautifully formed his lips were.

"I know it," she said, irritated with herself at how breathless her voice emerged.

It would never do for the Duke of Arse-ingham to know

she found him handsome. Or to discover the effect his nearness had on her. She would be mortified.

He regarded her solemnly, making heat creep through her. "Shall we?"

"Of course."

As one, they began to play. Addy would have expected them to be out of time, even slightly, and yet their fingers moved fluidly together, the melody effortlessly taking shape. And when it was time to sing, their voices blended melodiously. The duke's baritone was lovely, melding with her own voice.

Singing with Marchingham was a joy.

The realization alarmed her, one of her fingers slipping on the key and playing the wrong note. Quickly, she recovered, trying not to glance in the duke's direction. Trying to quell the heat creeping over her like the warmth of a July sun.

"*La terre est libre et le ciel est ouvert,*" they sang, and Addy couldn't resist stealing a peek at him.

It was a colossal mistake on her part. Because he was also looking at her, and their gazes met and held. It was as if a dam within her suddenly broke, unleashing a rushing torrent of emotions she had been frantically holding at bay.

A fluttering sensation began low in her belly. By the time they reached the crescendo of the final refrain, she couldn't look away.

"*Noël! Noël! Chantons le Rédempteur!*"

They played the final notes, and then the silence stretched, laden with what seemed a vast ocean of unspoken words. Addy's heart beat fast and hard. She didn't even like this man. Why was she so overcome with... What *was* it that she was feeling?

Longing?

Good heavens. Surely not. Her gaze settled on the

duke's lips. They were well-formed and unsmiling, his philtrum delightfully pronounced. His jaw was rigid. A mad, foolish notion struck her. She should kiss him. Kiss the Duke of Marchingham. Kiss the forbidding sternness from his lips.

The air between them crackled with something potent and indefinable.

"That was…pleasant, Miss Fox," he said with that unforgiving mouth.

His voice was still cold.

She blinked, forcing her stare from his mouth to his icy eyes. That was how he chose to describe what had passed between them during their duet? *Pleasant?*

Addy didn't like that. Not at all.

"Pleasant," she repeated.

"A nonsensical means of passing the time," he added, reverting to his haughty self.

"Do you know what's truly nonsensical, Your Graceship?" she asked, using the incorrect form of address she knew irked him. "The way you refuse to have any fun."

His nostrils flared. "It is merely *Your Grace*, madam, a fact which I suspect you know and yet continue to ignore so that you may irritate me. And I don't refuse to have fun. I am merely a man who shoulders too many burdens for frivolous amusements."

He wasn't wrong about the first part of what he had said. As for the second, it made her wonder just what his burdens were. Had she judged him too harshly?

Addy settled her hands in her lap, lacing her fingers together so that she wouldn't be tempted to reach for him. "I am but a confused Yankee, frustrated by your unfamiliar customs. You ought to take pity on me."

"Pity is the last thing I feel in regard to you, Miss Fox."

"Oh?" The fluttering sensation spread, moving through

the rest of her. "What *do* you feel in regard to me then, *Your Grace?*"

"Vexation."

His response was instant and biting.

She scowled at him. "Is that all?"

"Frustration."

"Do you like anyone, Marchingham?" she asked, trying to tamp down the disappointment rising within her at his words.

"Of course I do."

"Aside from yourself, I mean," she amended, unable to keep the sarcasm from her voice.

He bit out a short laugh, taking her by surprise. Mirth didn't seem like something the Duke of Marchingham would indulge in. Far too plebian. And yet, astoundingly, he had. And *she* had been the one to make him do it.

Addy grinned, ridiculously pleased by this development.

"You look far too happy for a woman who is about to find herself sleeping in the stables tonight," he said mildly, one ducal brow winging upward.

"Has the Duke of Marchingham just deigned to make a joke? Because if so, I will have to write to the newspapers. I'm sure it ought to be reported across the land. At the very least, it should be marked down upon an ancient scroll so that this sacred moment will forever be remembered."

He laughed again, and Addy found herself alarmingly affected by the way his smile transformed his face. His lips curved upward, and amusement gleamed in his eyes. She couldn't look away.

"Do you know, Miss Fox, that I've never met a woman capable of such astonishing insolence?" he asked conversationally.

Addy laughed. "I would be disappointed if you had. I consider myself an original."

His lips twitched. "Quite."

He was so proper and stiff-backed. Everything about him was perfection, from his neatly combed golden hair to his freshly shaven jaw, right down to his tweed trousers and coat and the well-shined leather of his boots. It made her long to muss his hair, to shock him. Addy told herself that was why she reached out, grasping a handful of his shirt, why she pulled him to her and sealed her lips to his, kissing the Duke of Marchingham.

# CHAPTER 5

*L*ion knew that either Miss Adelia Fox was a liar—or those half a dozen Swiss lads hadn't shown her a bloody thing about the art of kissing. Because she had frozen the moment her mouth pressed against his. Elation surged through him, along with a dizzying swell of desire. Her lips were soft and lush and silken.

They were just as he had thought they would be, only better. So much better.

He took control, cupping her nape and holding her to him, tenderly coaxing her into a response. Tentatively, she began kissing him back. Her actions were slow and hesitant at first, but she caught on swiftly, her lips chasing his.

Her scent enveloped him, sweetly floral. Kissing her was an intoxicating thrill, and now that he had her tempting mouth, he never wanted to stop. She made a throaty sound, part sigh, part moan, and he seized the opportunity to deepen the kiss, giving her his tongue. Her reaction was like an electric current straight down his spine. She opened for his exploration, pressing closer to him on the piano bench until her breasts were crushed into his chest.

Madness seized him.

Kissing Miss Fox was unlike any prior experience he'd had. She kissed him with the same unbridled enthusiasm she applied to her every action. Her kiss was uncontrolled and wild and yet somehow deliciously heady. Nothing about it was proper. This was the unrestrained, passionate kiss a mistress would give, not the refined peck a lady might allow a suitor.

Not that Lion was her suitor or that Miss Fox was a lady. He most definitely was *not* courting Miss Adelia Fox. He shouldn't even be kissing her. Indeed, he ought to have been appalled, yet he was the opposite. He was entranced. Obsessed. His cock had never been harder, and that was a most unwanted discovery.

But still, he didn't stop. He kissed her until he was breathless. Kissed her until he could scarcely remember his own name. Then he kissed her some more. He became attuned to her every breath and slight sigh, to the subtle pressure of her hand on his shoulder or her fingers grasping his shirtfront as if to hold him fast to her. She hadn't any need to worry on that score.

Lion wasn't going anywhere.

He was staying here on this blasted uncomfortable piano bench that had scarcely enough room for two, and his lips were never leaving Miss Fox's. As long as he continued kissing her, his mind couldn't be permitted to persuade him that what he was doing was wrong, ungentlemanly, and wholly improper. Because how could it be wrong when it felt so wonderfully, terrifyingly *right*?

When her tongue slid against his, he groaned. His sinful mind whirled with what he might do next. Kiss his way down her throat to feel the velvet-soft whisper of her skin on his lips? Or cup a breast through her bodice? It had been so long since he had last been consumed by passion. These days, he was too mired in duty and obligation to allow himself to feel. And oh, how good it felt to be reckless, just this once. To taste this woman on his lips. To suck her tongue and make her whimper. To kiss her until she arched her lush, full breasts into his chest and threaded her fingers through his hair. Her nails scraped his scalp, and God, it felt wondrous, like the unlocking of a door deep within himself.

He nipped her lip and then strung a path of kisses along her jaw, eager to learn every part of her that he could. Her breath fell hot and rushed on his cheek, the smallest of intimacies and yet so very decadent. To be this near. To have her hairpins at the mercy of his eager fingers as he plucked them free from her coiffure, sending her golden mane tumbling down her back. To drink her scent into his lungs. To nuzzle her temple, to kiss her ear as she trembled.

The things he wanted to do to her. To do with her. To show her. He was drunk on lust. On her. She clutched at him, tipping her head back and making an erotic sound of enjoyment that had his ballocks tightening. He'd never been this tempted by mere kisses. Nor had he ever been more undone. He was at her sensual mercy. She may not have learned how to kiss from those Swiss suitors, but she had certainly learned how to ensnare him.

The sudden and distant closing of a door somewhere beyond the music room brought Lion back to himself with a jolt, pulling him from the edge of ruin. This was *Miss Fox* he was kissing. He had to stop.

Reluctantly, Lion tore his mouth from hers. Her green eyes were wide, her lips swollen from his kisses and darkened to the shade of summer berry compote. Her breathing was every bit as ragged as his, her breasts rising and falling from her uneven gasps. She looked as dazed as he felt and unfairly beautiful, too.

He swallowed hard. "My actions were most regrettable.

Please accept my sincere apology for behaving in a manner so unbecomingly forward."

She licked her lips. "No."

Lion tried not to stare at her mouth. "No?"

"I refuse to accept your apology. Why should you be sorry? I'm not."

She was equal parts mesmerizing and infuriating. Of course she wasn't sorry. Miss Fox likely did whatever she wanted whenever the notion took her, regardless of aught else.

"It won't happen again, I assure you," he added stiffly.

What was wrong with him? Why had he kissed Miss Fox? And why was he so damned attracted to her? He had known beautiful women in his past. There was nothing unique about the hoyden American who had invaded his serenity with her bold presence.

"If you say so, Your Graceship," she said in a breathless tone.

And then she had the temerity to wink at him, as if she were humoring his assertion and she didn't believe him for a moment.

"It won't," he insisted.

Because he intended to keep his distance from Miss Fox for the rest of her stay here at Marchingham Hall. Obviously, he could not trust himself where she was concerned. The temptation was far too great.

Before she could convey further protest, he rose from the piano bench and offered her a hasty bow. "I'll leave you to your music, Miss Fox."

As he strode away, he licked his lips, and he tasted *her*.

And he wanted more.

Good God.

❋

"It's a terrible shame that there isn't a tree or at the very least some festoons," Addy lamented to Aunt Pearl that evening as they sat before a crackling fire in the library. "It's as bleak as winter in this house. I cannot fathom such a grim lack of cheer."

Dandy was snuggled on her lap, peaceful and lightly snoring. Reports from the stable earlier that day indicated that the snow had yet to melt, meaning that roads might not become passable again until a fortnight had passed.

They were still, quite possibly, going to be stranded with the duke for Christmas.

Marchingham had been conspicuously absent at dinner. After those scorching kisses in the music room, Addy didn't know what she had expected of him. But it certainly hadn't been for him to retreat and hide himself away.

Not after the passionate way he had kissed her.

*Do not think of it now, Addy*, she inwardly admonished herself, even though those heated music room moments had furthermost occupied her mind every second since the duke's mouth had left hers. He was excellent at kissing, which she supposed was to be expected since everything about the Duke of Marchingham was utter, unparalleled perfection except for the shabby state of his manor house. Addy rather wished he had been wet-lipped and oafish and that his breath had smelled of herrings and pickles and moldy cheese.

It would have made everything so much easier.

"Your mother decorates for Christmas more than anyone I know," Aunt Pearl pointed out mildly, interrupting Addy's thoughts. "With the duke the only one in residence, I can understand his not wanting the fuss. Besides, I sincerely doubt there are enough servants to contend with such a formidable task."

That much was true. For such a grand house, Marchingham Hall was woefully lacking in domestics. Addy had noticed it at once. Of course, back at home, Mama kept more servants than any other household in the city as a point of pride and a symbol of the Fox family's immense wealth.

"Mama would be horrified by the absence of trimmings," Addy agreed.

"Speaking of your mother, what do you think she will say when she learns of your latest scrape?" Aunt Pearl asked shrewdly.

Addy bit her lip. "Do we need to tell her?"

Aunt Pearl gave her a meaningful look over the gold rims of her spectacles. "I don't dare keep secrets from her. You know how she is."

She sighed. "Yes, I do."

Mama was notoriously unforgiving. Once, she had banished Aunt Pearl from paying calls to their Fifth Avenue mansion for an entire year because her aunt had failed to tell her mother in a sufficiently timely manner that Mrs. Richard Thomas Taylor had been spreading gossip about her. Papa had taken to visiting Aunt Pearl instead, and he'd graciously included Addy in his clandestine visits. She had kept her silence about the matter, naturally. No one wanted to be on the wrong side of Mrs. Cornelius Fox. Not even her own family.

"Then we must inform her that you were not invited to Marchingham Hall as you claimed," Aunt Pearl said, her voice uncharacteristically stern.

"But Mama will likely be furious with me for my subterfuge," Addy argued stubbornly. "Do you truly want me to suffer her wrath?"

"You are her flesh and blood. Better for you to suffer her wrath than me. Need I remind you of the incident with Mrs. Richard Thomas Taylor?"

She sighed, and Dandy opened one chocolate-brown eye

to peer curiously up at her. "All is well, my darling sweet pea," she crooned, petting Dandy's silken head.

"Adelia Louise?" Aunt Pearl prodded her.

Addy blew out an exasperated breath and pinned her aunt with an aggrieved look. "You know I dislike it when you call me that. Adelia and Louise do not go together well. Not at all."

"That is precisely why I call you Adelia Louise. It captures your attention every time."

Addy grumbled beneath her breath.

"What was that, my dear?"

"Nothing," she said, offering her aunt a bright smile.

Her aunt gave her a knowing look. "You never answered my question."

"I recall Mama's petty fury with you over Mrs. Richard Thomas Taylor. It was very badly done of Mama. She knows what a wretched gossip Mrs. Taylor is. The woman can't open her mouth without saying something awful about someone else. And it wasn't as if you indulged in her nonsense."

"I put the terrible woman in her place," Aunt Pearl agreed stoutly. "But I heard the gossip on a Tuesday, and I failed to tell your mother until a Thursday. It was an egregious sin she couldn't possibly forgive."

"So you see why we mustn't tell her about my little fib?" Addy tried hopefully.

"I see why we *must*. You are her daughter. She will forgive you before a year is over."

Dandy raised her head and made a half woof that heralded someone about to enter the room. Addy glanced toward the door just as Marchingham appeared there. Dandy gave a full bark and leapt from Addy's lap, racing across the carpets in her customary stiff-legged prowl. Although a small dog, Dandy possessed the bravado of a hound three times her size.

"Dandy acts as if she is a lioness about to tear apart her prey," Aunt Pearl observed in a quiet aside.

"That is because no one has ever told her she is little, so she thinks she's the size of a bear," Addy said.

"Halt," ordered the duke.

And to Addy's astonishment, Dandy stopped before him and sat down, as calmly as if she had been following Marchingham's edicts all her life.

The duke reached into his pocket and extracted something small, tossing it to Dandy, who eagerly caught it in her jaws and swallowed it down.

"What are you feeding my dog?" Addy demanded, outraged.

"Cheese," he said, his demeanor and tone as grim as if he had just announced a death instead of elaborating upon the treat he had just fed Dandy.

Then he sketched an elegant bow, as if he were in a ballroom. Even his *bows* were perfection, for heaven's sake.

"Oh," she said, her ire instantly deflating. "I was hoping it wasn't poison."

He gave her a scathing look as he straightened to his formidable height. "Do you think I would harm your mongrel?"

"You wanted her to sleep in the stables," Addy pointed out. "Dandy, come here. You ought not to accept cheese from the enemy."

Aunt Pearl chuckled. "It looks as if His Grace has a new admirer."

Dandy was indeed gazing up at the duke in an adoring manner, ignoring Addy's entreaty.

Marchingham reached into his pocket and extracted

another small lump of cheese, tossing it to Dandy, who eagerly devoured it.

Addy glared at him, trying not to think about how his lips had felt upon hers, masterful and smooth and demanding. Nor how much she had liked his kisses.

"I do believe you are bribing my dog," she said. "How did you know she likes cheese?"

"All dogs like cheese."

"I thought you didn't like dogs. How would you know anything about them?"

He gave her a hooded stare. "I had a dog myself once when I was a lad."

A hint of sorrow laced his voice. There was something to that story, and she found herself longing to know.

"Would you care to join us, Your Grace?" Aunt Pearl interjected cheerfully. "Addy and I were enjoying the warmth of your fire and admiring your library's vast collection of books. We did so miss you at dinner."

"*Aunt Pearl* missed you at dinner," Addy corrected. "I hadn't even noticed you weren't there."

"Adelia Louise," her aunt scolded quietly at her side.

She was being rude and she knew it, but she was rather nettled that Marchingham had avoided dinner after kissing her so passionately, only to reappear this evening and woo her beloved dog with cheese. And with *pocket cheese*! It was hardly ducal to go about carrying cheddar in one's coat. She couldn't think he ordinarily did so.

"I did notice after Aunt Pearl commented upon it," she added with feigned sweetness.

"I am dismayed that my presence is so easily overlooked," he said stiffly, his gaze meeting hers.

Had she hurt his feelings? She couldn't tell. His face was unreadable. She hadn't supposed he could be so easily offended. He seemed quite inured to her at all times.

Except for when he had been kissing her.

Addy banished the wicked thought.

He strode past Dandy, entering the library fully, dashing Addy's hope that he would excuse himself and leave her to her peace with Aunt Pearl. Dandy followed at his heels as if she were loyally trailing after Addy.

All because of pocket cheese and one cunning duke.

"Apparently your presence isn't easily overlooked by *someone*," Addy said with a pointed look in her beloved dog's direction. "To think I have been replaced in her affections all because of a few hunks of cheese from your pocket. It was likely covered in lint."

His lips twitched as he seated himself in the empty chair at her side. "I must admit, I'm wounded by your poor opinion of the state of my pockets, Miss Fox. I can assure you that they never hold anything as disagreeable as lint."

Dandy sat at his feet, gazing at him with her big brown eyes, silently begging for more pocket cheese.

"Traitor," she grumbled at her dog.

"I prefer to think of her as having discerning taste."

"Do you? Hmm, I rather like to call it having no loyalty. Who saved her from a frigid end in the stables?"

"Who saved her from a frigid end in the carriage?" Aunt Pearl added.

"You, of course," Addy conceded. "I'll forever be in your debt for rescuing my darling Dandy."

"By that logic, you are also in my debt, Miss Fox," Marchingham drawled.

Drat the man.

"Perhaps you have already collected what you are owed," she dared, keeping a tranquil smile in place.

Addy was referring to what had transpired in the music room, of course. There was nothing she wanted more than to shock a response out of him. How could he have kissed her as he had, only to reemerge with such elegant nonchalance, as if her presence were of no consequence to him?

He reached into his coat. "I don't think I have."

Surely he didn't have *more* pocket cheese, did he? Dandy wriggled with excitement, then licked her chops.

"Stay sitting," Marchingham ordered Dandy in a voice that was authoritative and yet far from sharp. "Behave, little mongrel."

"Dandy is *not* a mongrel," Addy countered, insulted on her dog's behalf.

He extracted another small hunk of cheese, not answering her. As the duke lowered his hand toward Dandy, Addy was compelled to warn him.

"Take care when you feed her, Marchingham. She has very sharp teeth, and she tends to bite."

His blue gaze burned into her. "It would seem that she has a great deal in common with her mistress, in that case."

Addy's mouth fell open at the jibe and the way Dandy gently took the piece of cheese from the duke's fingers, rather than ravenously devouring it along with a few bits of his flesh.

"Are you intending to vex me at every turn?" she demanded.

Aunt Pearl coughed delicately. "The hour is late. I do believe it is past time for me to retire. Addy, do you care to join me?"

"Of course, Aunt Pearl. I'll take Dandy for her small walk in the gardens first and then retire for the evening as well."

Her aunt rose from her seat and pushed her spectacles up the bridge of her nose. "Good evening to you both."

As Aunt Pearl began to take her leave of the library, Addy turned her attention back to her stubbornly treacherous dog. Dandy was still seated before Marchingham, giving him her undivided attention.

"Come to me, Dandy," she ordered the pup.

Dandy refused to comply. Instead, she rose on her hind legs and placed her paws on the duke's knees and gave a small bark. Addy was familiar with her dog's forms of communication by now. She knew what Dandy was requesting—more pocket cheese.

"Come along, you naughty girl. No more cheese for you today, pocket or otherwise."

The duke surprised her by patting Dandy gently on the head. "Her name was Mittens."

He was gazing down at Dandy, stroking her sleek fur, seemingly lost somewhere in his own thoughts. Marchingham was telling her about his dog, she realized.

"Mittens," she repeated. "You must have been a very young lad to have named a dog so frivolously. I would have thought her name would be Queen or Princess or something equally lofty."

"I was four, and I don't expect I was sufficiently lofty just yet," he said with a small smile, glancing in Addy's direction even as he continued patting the dog's head.

Somehow, the thought of him as a little boy made her heart soften. Had he always been proper and staid and serious, even then? Or had his life experiences and his duties molded him into the man he was today? She desperately wanted the answers to these questions. These, and so many more.

"You were fond of Mittens?" she asked hesitantly.

"I was." He stroked Dandy's head yet again, his countenance turning contemplative. "For three years, she was my favorite companion. She was forever at my heels, following me wherever I went. Until one day, she wasn't."

"What happened to her?" she asked, dread cramping her stomach.

His gaze returned to hers, his eyes sad. "She was struck by

a cart in London. She wandered from the house without anyone taking note until it was too late."

"Oh, Marchingham." Her heart ached for the dog taken too soon, for the young boy he must have been. "That's truly awful. I'm so sorry that happened. You must have been inconsolable."

"My father…didn't tolerate weeping, and particularly not over a mere dog." Marchingham swallowed. "I was punished for the excessive emotion I exhibited and was never allowed another hound."

What manner of man would reprimand his young son for being sad that his beloved pup had been killed? Addy was horrified. No wonder the duke was so reserved and frigid. He had been raised that way, and then he had taken over his ducal duties at an early age when his father had died. Addy knew that much from what Letty and Lila had told her. They had been girls of seven and eight at the time, their older brother only eighteen. His revelations certainly put his reaction to Dandy in a different light.

Before she could think twice, she reached for him, settling her hand over his on the armrest of his chair. A jolt skipped up her arm and slid down her spine. Touching him had been a mistake. He turned to her, their gazes colliding, and it was as if the bottom of her stomach dropped out. In his eyes, she saw the man within Marchingham's frosty, impenetrable exterior. She saw the same man who had kissed her until she'd been breathless.

And she longed for that man.

Addy leaned toward him, wanting to kiss him, to banish the unpleasant memories haunting him, to give him comfort. Wanting things she should never want from the Duke of Marchingham, who had made no secret of his scathing disapproval of her.

But he hadn't seemed nearly so disapproving when his mouth had been on hers in the music room.

"That is dreadfully unfair," she said, her voice thick.

"Life is unfair, Miss Fox," he countered, his head angling toward hers.

It was as if they were magnets, drawn together. Marchingham turned his hand so that their palms were aligned, their fingers entwined. Addy was suddenly hot everywhere, but not because of the hearty fire.

"I suppose it is," she allowed, unable to look away from his eyes.

Was he thinking about what had happened between them? Was he wanting more too?

"Miss Fox," Marchingham began, only to be interrupted by a determined bark from Dandy.

Dandy pawed at the duke's knee, apparently jealous and seeking his undivided attention. Addy bit the inner corner of her lip and considered her dog. *That makes two of us, Dandy*, she thought grimly.

Marchingham withdrew his hand, using it instead to point at Dandy in an authoritative fashion. "Sit, Dandy."

Dandy promptly settled on the carpet, gazing up at him adoringly.

Addy clearly needed to procure some cheese, though she hadn't a pocket to store it in. Marchingham withdrew yet another hunk and tossed it to Dandy, who caught it in her mouth and swallowed it whole.

"Little beggar," Addy said without sting, deciding that it was past time for her to flee the duke's presence before she did anything reckless.

Like kiss him again.

She rose from her chair. "Come, Dandy. A quick stop outdoors, and then it's time for rest."

The duke stood as well, his full height overwhelming

Addy. When he was seated, it was easy to forget how wonderfully tall he was.

He offered her an elegant half bow. "Good evening, Miss Fox."

His formality felt wrong. But she knew that clinging to it was for the best. They could forget the music room had ever happened. It was apparent that Marchingham didn't wish to revisit their lapse in judgment. He hadn't even spoken of it.

"Good evening, Your Grace," she returned, because, like his formality, needling him about his form of address felt wrong. "Come, Dandelion."

Dandy looked from Marchingham to Addy.

"Go on," he told Dandy.

And as if she had been awaiting his permission, Dandy finally turned away and trotted to Addy. Hastily, she retreated from the library, thinking grimly that somehow, both she and her dog had been charmed by the Duke of Marchingham.

She wished for a miracle, that the snow would melt entirely tomorrow.

Because the sooner she could leave Marchingham Hall and the handsome duke who presided over it, the better.

## CHAPTER 6

Lion trudged through the snow in the frozen gardens at Marchingham Hall. The air bore a stinging chill. The sun was hidden behind leaden clouds, and flakes were beginning to fall anew, covering the tremendous amount that had already blanketed the land a week ago in the storm that had brought Miss Adelia Fox to his door.

Well, to be specific, Lion himself had been responsible for bringing the maddening hoyden to his door. But it was Miss Fox's fault that she had been in such a precarious position in the first place, huddled in the fleeting warmth given from the heated brick at her feet in a mired carriage, about to perish in a snowstorm.

Regardless of the reason, she had been in residence at Marchingham Hall for the last seven days, tempting him with her sunny smile and her stubborn attempts at persuading him that he must decorate for Christmas. Seven days of turning a corner in his own house and discovering the faintest trace of violet and orris root that meant she was somewhere near and seeking her out despite himself. A whole week of her little dog following him about as if she had been his loyal companion for years. Miss Fox vowed the hound's steadfast adoration was down to the pocket cheese he continually offered her.

Lion thought otherwise. He and Dandy had simply... bonded.

He had forgotten what it felt like to experience the unfettered devotion of a hound. The French bulldog was quite possibly as mad as Miss Fox was, and yet Lion couldn't help but find himself liking them both. Far too much.

And unfortunately for him, it looked as if his unexpected guests would be forced to stay at Marchingham Hall for even longer. Another week, perhaps, if the weather refused to warm and the snow would not melt.

He sighed, and then the happy bark of Dandy cut through the quiet of the snow-covered landscape. Lion turned to find a black blur racing toward him. Dandy adored racing about in the snow. He couldn't lie—so much exuberance never failed to lighten his mood.

"Halt, Cerberus," he commanded wryly, using the pet name he often used for Dandelion, much to Miss Fox's irritation.

Two could play at the game of nettling, he'd discovered.

The dog came to a stop at his feet, her mouth open to reveal a line of startlingly white, sharp teeth, her tongue lolling. She must have exhausted herself. But where was Miss Fox?

"Dandy," Miss Fox called as if on cue, rounding a hedge and then stopping when she caught sight of Lion.

She was bundled up heavily, the cold painting her cheeks a becoming shade of pink.

"Your Grace," she said, her voice breathless. "Forgive me for nearly bowling you over. I was rushing after Dandy. She was having one of her happy bouts, you see. One moment, she was burying her face in the snow and eating it, and the next she was tearing away into the maze. I could scarcely keep up with her."

Dandy's face was indeed coated in white.

"Your dog is madder than a Bedlamite," he commented before reaching into his pocket and withdrawing a small chunk of cheese. "Sit, Cerberus."

Dandy obliged, her brown eyes fixed upon the treat he held.

"Her name is Sweet Miss Dandelion Mae, not Cerberus," Miss Fox grumbled.

"She answers to both," Lion pointed out, ignoring the ludicrous name the woman had given her dog.

"She doesn't resemble a hideous three-headed dog monster in the slightest."

Only Miss Fox would stand in the snow, arguing with him about such a topic. Lion wanted to kiss her again. He hadn't. Not since his folly in the music room. He had been able to make certain that they were never alone, aside from the evening in the library when he had unburdened himself to her.

About Mittens, of all things.

His sire must be rolling in his grave.

"She is fearsome in her own way," he argued, giving Dandy the cheese she was after.

She caught it before it fell in the snow, swallowing it down.

"Does she ever chew?" he wondered aloud.

"Not when she particularly loves a food."

"Her manners are appalling." His gaze strayed from the hound to Miss Fox.

It didn't matter how many times he looked upon her. Each time, he felt a sudden rush of awareness and appreciation that only grew stronger with the days that passed.

Miss Fox smiled at him. "Her judgment is occasionally lacking where certain matters are concerned. Matters such as who she favors."

Lion couldn't quell his laugh. "In that regard, I'm persuaded that her judgment is nothing short of impeccable."

"You would."

They stared at each other. Despite the cold, he found warmth spreading through him. Miss Adelia Fox was wrong for him in every way. She was boisterous, ridiculous, and spoiled. He was reasonably certain she was incapable of reserve. She most certainly had none of the polish to be expected in a duchess. And besides all that, she was an American. A wayward hoyden who may or may not have kissed her way out of a Swiss finishing school.

He cleared his throat. "We should go inside. Surely you and the little mongrel are cold."

"You know she isn't a mongrel," Miss Fox huffed just as he had known she would. "She is—"

"Born of the finest bloodlines in Paris, et cetera, et cetera," he interrupted. "We ought to make haste before the snow begins to fall in truth."

"Do you know what I dearly loved to do whenever it snowed when I was a girl?" Miss Fox asked.

"Vex your governesses until they ran from their posts, wailing and gnashing their teeth?" he guessed uncharitably.

She gave him a chastising look. "Of course not. My governess adored me. I was the most well-behaved girl ever in her charge."

He chortled. "Were you then also the *only* girl ever in her charge?"

Her eyes narrowed. "Of course not, Your Graceship."

Suddenly, Dandy, who had been behaving beautifully in hopes of more pocket cheese, barked and ran off down the path, sending snow flying in her wake as her paws dashed through the snow.

"Dandy! Come back here, you naughty girl." Miss Fox made to chase after her dog.

Lion stopped her, laying a gloved hand on her sleeve. "I'll go. I have pocket cheese."

Without awaiting her response, he chased after Dandy, who was apparently experiencing yet another of her *happy bouts*, bounding through the snow with frenzied enthusiasm as she panted and her tongue lolled.

"Dandy, cheese," he called.

The hound spun about so quickly that she rolled in the snow. The moment she was on all four paws again, she rushed back to him, anticipating her prize.

"Manners," he cautioned.

Dandy sat, having spent the past week learning various new commands from him. He had enjoyed himself far more than he could bear to admit.

Lion tossed Dandy her scrap of cheese, and he was about to encourage her to follow him back to where they had come from when a lump of snow suddenly smacked him in the arm. He stared down at the white coating his sleeve, then looked up to find a grinning Miss Fox. She had snow on her gloves.

The minx had thrown a snowball at him.

"You never let me finish telling you what I loved to do when I was a girl," she said, as if that explained her actions.

It didn't. At least, not to Lion.

He blinked, his mind struggling to make sense of the woman.

"Snowball fights," she elaborated. "I loved having snowball fights in the gardens whenever it snowed. Of course, then I grew older, and Mama told me it wasn't ladylike to throw snow at anyone."

"I can see that you heeded her sage advice."

She laughed. "I simply waited until she wasn't at home to do it."

"Ah," he said, staring at her, bemused.

When Miss Fox smiled, she was breathtakingly lovely. How would he possibly continue to resist this insane attraction he felt for her until the snow melted? Perhaps *he* was going to have to be the one to bed down in the stables.

"Have you ever had a snowball fight?" she asked.

"Of course not."

There had been no room for frivolity in his childhood. And then, when he'd been little more than a child himself, the obligations of the dukedom had fallen upon him. He had inherited not just the title, but all the debts and duties that came along with it, and his sisters, too.

"You have no notion what you've been missing," said the mad Miss Fox.

Just before she bent down, scooped up a ball of snow, and hurled it at him.

This time, she hit him directly in the center of his chest.

Dandy bit at the snowball as it disintegrated and fell to the ground, making a game of it. Then she had a *happy bout* back to Miss Fox, before whirling through the snow and burying her face in it.

"I wonder how it was even possible for you to have found a hound who is every bit as outrageous as you are," he mused.

Miss Fox's response was to launch yet another ball of snow at him. This one faltered a bit and hit him on the lower leg.

"Another hit," she exclaimed. "I'm currently the victor by a score of three to zero. If you hope to have a chance of winning, you'll need to at least try, Marchingham."

He couldn't. Could he? No. Of course not. All the training he had received—most of which had been instilled in him with a strong birching from his father—refused to allow him to stoop so low.

"It isn't done to fling snow at ladies."

"I'm not a lady." With unabashed glee, she scooped up some more snow.

And it occurred to Lion that he could stand there like an oafish lump and continue to accept her pummeling, or he could defend himself.

He *could*.

He found himself snatching up a handful of snow and molding it into a ball just in time for another of Miss Fox's missiles to strike his left arm. He took aim and threw, hitting his target—her bodice. She laughed and their battle began in truth, Miss Fox hastening to make another snowball as Lion ducked and dodged, landing several blows to her person as she made her fair share of hits. Before long, they were both laughing, scrambling for snow, hurling it as quickly as they could. Dandy ran between them, trying to catch the snowballs in midair.

Their battle lasted for the better part of a quarter hour, until they were both covered in snow. Finally, Lion held up his empty hands. "We ought to go inside and warm up before we take a chill."

"One more," Miss Fox said stubbornly, revealing a snowball she'd hidden behind her back.

It hit him squarely in the hat, knocking it from his head and sending snow raining into his face. Without a second of hesitation, he formed another snowball and sent it in her direction, also striking her hat. Because her hat must have been pinned in place, the snowball fell over her face, leaving her sputtering.

"You scoundrel!"

She laughed, spitting snow.

By God, the woman was glorious.

His week of trying to see her as little as possible had only left him desperate for more of her. The effect had been the opposite of his intention. And now, here they were, covered in snow, and all he wanted was to kiss her again. To feel her smile on his own lips. To drink in some of her sunshine and allow it to warm his wintry heart.

He was walking toward her without even realizing it.

"Forgive me," he said as he reached her. "I didn't intend for that to happen."

Her eyes sparkled with mirth. "You didn't intend to hit my hat with a snowball?"

"No, I quite meant to do that." He removed a glove and wiped the snow from her cheeks with the backs of his fingers.

Her skin was smooth and soft. Lion swallowed hard against a sudden, stunning rush of desire. He stroked down her throat, over her nose, her forehead. Gently brushed away the wisps of hair curling at her temples. There was no snow remaining, only a trace of wetness, and he couldn't stop touching her.

"Thank you," Miss Fox said, sounding breathless.

Somewhere behind him, Dandy was running about in the snow. The sounds of her grunting and panting did nothing to overpower his wildly beating heart. His fingers moved with a mind of their own, tracing over the Cupid's bow of her upper lip.

"I seem to have missed a spot," he murmured, lowering his head toward hers.

"You did?"

"Yes. Here."

And then he covered her mouth with his. It was a terrible idea. Wholly inadvisable. Exactly what he had spent the last week avoiding. And it felt so bloody good he could scarcely bear it.

Her lips parted, and he deepened the kiss, tasting tea and sweet strawberry preserves she must have slathered on a scone earlier, and something else that was mysteriously, indefinably Adelia Fox. The sweetest elixir he had ever known. He cupped her cheek tenderly, taking his time to learn her mouth, drinking in her soft sigh as his tongue stroked against hers.

She clutched at his shoulders, holding him to her as if she feared he would flee. But she needn't have worried. Her lips were intoxicating. He couldn't get enough of them. And her body? It was a dream. His free hand fell on her waist, pulling her flush against him, bringing the fullness of her breasts into his chest. How desperately he longed to peel away her layers. To tear at her silk, velvet, and wool until she was bared to his feverish gaze. To kiss and taste every inch of this ravishing, vexing, wonderful woman.

But that was foolish and impossible. They were standing in the midst of the outdoors, the punishing winter wind whirling about, snowflakes falling around them. And still, he kissed her. Kissed her because he couldn't shake the restless feeling that he *had* to. That his mouth on hers was imperative.

She wound her arms around his neck. Snow fell on his head, and he didn't care. He was dimly aware of Dandy jumping at his legs, attempting to insert herself. The little mongrel was always desperate for attention. But he hadn't any to spare. Miss Fox owned all of it just now.

Her lips clung to his, responding so sweetly, as if she were every bit as desperate for him as he was for her. Her tongue dueled with his, and he delighted in her boldness. Nothing Miss Adelia Fox did was meek or mild. She was brazen in all ways, and it both horrified him and drew him to her. He shouldn't want her.

But he couldn't stop himself.

He eased a path of kisses along her jaw, then down the sleek column of her throat, finding her pulse with his lips. And then because he couldn't resist, he opened his mouth, tasting her soft skin, reveling in her swift inhalation. He breathed deeply, taking in the soft floral scent of her, unable to get enough.

Dandy chose that moment to bark loudly, bringing Lion back to his senses with a jolt. He was sucking on Miss Adelia Fox's throat like a green lad who was about to have his first experience with a woman. Lion withdrew, stepping back from her as if he'd been scalded.

"Forgive me," he bit out, all he could manage.

Dandy barked.

Lion didn't even bother to retrieve his fallen hat. He fled the gardens like a coward.

# CHAPTER 7

The hour was indecently late, and there was no reason for Addy to hover outside the Duke of Marchingham's bedchamber except a scandalous one. But when had she ever balked at causing a little scandal if it meant having her way?

Never, of course.

Her hand hovered, her determination overshadowed by her fear of rejection. This was her last chance to take the greatest risk of her life. All she needed was to muster the courage to knock on the duke's door.

The snow had finally melted sufficiently so that the roads were once again passable. In the morning, Addy, Alfred, and Aunt Pearl would be leaving. A week and a half had passed from the time Addy had unceremoniously arrived at Marchingham Hall to this evening.

And in that time, everything had changed.

She and Marchingham had fallen into a pattern. He hid himself away, only to occasionally emerge, kiss her breathless, and then apologize and disappear again. They had kissed in the music room, the gardens, the library, and even once in the hall, where anyone could have happened upon them. Each time, he withdrew, only to pretend as if nothing had occurred between them when their paths crossed next.

She had never met a man more frustrating. It was as if there were two different dukes. One was cold and aloof and proper, and the other was passionate and reckless.

The latter was, naturally, Addy's preference. She liked when those glimmers of his wicked self emerged. She wanted more of them. She wanted to muss his hair. To climb into his lap and kiss him until her lips ached. To melt every last trace of his ice. She wanted to hold his hand and to have more snowball fights. To make him laugh. To win his smiles.

And perhaps even to win his heart.

That last realization had brought her here, to the room she had discovered was his, at nearly midnight. Her time was running out. At dinner, Marchingham had been painstakingly polite, haughty, and reserved. When she had spoken of the plans she and Aunt Pearl had made to leave for the train station in the morning, he hadn't even blinked.

What if his lack of reaction was because he would be relieved to rid himself of her uninvited presence at his home?

What if he had only kissed her out of boredom?

What if a man could kiss a woman yet also despise her and consider her desperately beneath him?

What if her foolish—and false—bragging about kissing half a dozen Swiss lads during her escape from finishing school had persuaded him that she hadn't any virtue?

The questions went on and on.

And on.

Addy took a deep, fortifying breath and, raising her hand, poised to knock at last.

Her insidious mind, however, refused to allow her a

reprieve. It started whirling anew with a fresh round of questions.

What if her presence at his bedroom this late at night would horrify him?

What if—?

The door suddenly opened, halting all further thought. For a moment, she could do nothing more than stare at the sight of Marchingham in a dark silk dressing gown. Her breath caught in her lungs. She, who prided herself on never faltering or lacking an opinion, stood speechless in the hall, admiring the lamplight's gilded glints in his wavy hair. Their gazes clashed and held.

"Miss Fox." His brows drew together, his confusion apparent. "Is something amiss?"

"Addy," she blurted.

He continued to stare, his expression inscrutable.

She took another deep breath. "I wish you would call me Addy, not Miss Fox."

He was the first to blink. "That would be far too familiar of me."

"More familiar than your mouth on mine?" she countered, summoning all the bravado she possessed. "I hardly think so."

Marchingham said nothing. He simply stood there in his dressing gown, looking unfairly handsome. Looking perfect. Not even a hair was out of place. He didn't look like a man about to retire for the night. He looked like a gentleman about to attend a ball, if not for the dressing gown and his bare feet.

At the reminder that he wore no shoes, her gaze slipped to the floor. His feet were long and large and not at all hairy like Papa's were. In fact, they were quite lovely, as far as feet were concerned. Not that Addy was a foot connoisseur, that was. But she could now say with unhesitating certitude that the Duke of Marchingham's feet were every bit as handsome as the rest of him.

"I have been remiss," Marchingham began.

"Do you like kissing me?" she asked at the same time.

He swallowed, and because she had wrested her gaze back to his face, she tracked the bob of his Adam's apple, fascinated by how masculine his throat was. How she longed to lay her lips there. To kiss his neck as he had hers that day in the snowy garden. To taste his skin as she had his mouth.

"That is hardly the sort of question a lady ought to ask a gentleman," he pointed out, his voice low and smooth.

He didn't sound shocked or scandalized or even displeased. Rather, he sounded intrigued.

"We have already established that I'm not a lady." She drew upon her mettle, summoning her sunniest smile. "And I take note that you haven't provided me with an answer either."

A lone brow rose. "I am certain you already have your answer."

Did he truly think she would allow him to escape her with such ease this time? Addy knew him by now.

She shook her head. "I want to hear it from you."

The air hung heavy with portent. Addy couldn't shake the feeling that no moment in her life would ever compare to this one. One wrong word, one false step, and Marchingham would run from her again. He would likely retreat into his bedroom and bar the door, not emerging until he saw the back of her heading down the approach to Marchingham Hall.

Something shifted in his expression, the sternness fading, his jaw relaxing. "I shouldn't enjoy it."

"But you do," she pressed.

He inclined his head. "Yes."

Elation shot through her, almost making her giddy.

"I'm leaving in the morning."

His lips compressed, the harsh angle of his jaw tightening again. "I am aware of that, madam."

"Then perhaps you will call me by my name."

"Adelia Louise."

He had remembered her middle name. The realization sent warmth creeping through her.

"Addy," she countered.

Anyone could call her Adelia, just as anyone might know she was Adelia Louise Fox. The newspapers had reported on everything from the size of her waist to the color of her eyes, to the size of the fortune her father had settled upon her as a lure for prospective husbands. She hated the public perception of her, the ceaseless desire from people she had never met to know about her. To think they knew her merely because they had read about her in the papers.

But not everyone had leave to call her Addy. That name was reserved for her closest family and friends. She wanted to hear it now, in the duke's precise, perfectly accented baritone. Just once. More than once, if she were ruthlessly honest with herself, but once would suffice if it was all she could be allotted.

Marchingham swallowed again, looking as if he were at war with himself. So handsome and composed, and yet there was a storm gathering in his eyes. The same storm she had felt in him when he'd taken her in his arms and kissed her, when his tongue had slipped inside her mouth, when he had held her to him as if she were something both precious and breakable all at once.

"Say it," she urged him. "Or are you too afraid that saying it will make everything that has happened between us these last eleven days impossible to ignore?"

"Addy," he bit out, as if doing so caused him physical pain.

"Addy Louise Fox, you should know better than to be knocking at an unwed gentleman's door at midnight."

She grinned at him, unable to contain the wild rush of joy coursing through her. She felt like a fireworks display in the night sky, explosive and combustible.

"I do know better."

He frowned, his nostrils flaring. "Then why are you here?"

"You know why."

"Addy," he rasped, clearly trying to cling to his resolve.

But then he reached for her, and she knew he was failing. His hands clamped on her waist in a possessive grip as she stepped forward. Their bodies connected from chest to hip. And oh, without the layers she ordinarily wore, what a revelation it was. She could feel him against her—that male part of him, thick and insistent against her stomach.

Proof he was not unaffected, had she needed any.

"What shall I call you?" she asked, settling one hand on his shoulder while the other cupped his cheek.

Letty and Lila had always referred to him as Marchingham. She had no notion what his given name was, even if she did know the taste of him on her lips and the way he kissed.

"You shouldn't call me anything."

But despite his warning, he turned his head, punctuating his words with a kiss directly to the center of her palm.

More warmth spread through her. She liked that. She liked that very, very much.

"Tell me," she whispered.

"I loathe my name," he murmured. "I always have."

"What is it? I promise not to laugh."

Her teasing had its intended effect, startling a chuckle out of him.

"Hoyden."

She feigned an innocent look. "Your given name is Hoyden? I do agree it's rather unusual."

"No, *you* are a hoyden." His tone was gruff, but there was no bite to it, no sting. "My name is Lionel, but I prefer Lion."

It suited him. Powerful and regal and dangerous, all at once.

"Lion," she repeated softly, liking the way it felt on her lips.

Liking what it meant. The Duke of Marchingham had told her his given name. And he was holding her in his arms. He hadn't pushed her away or denied her. He hadn't fled or withdrawn.

*Yet*, reminded an inner voice sharply. *Give him time to realize the error of his ways, and he will retreat as if all of Hades is at his heels.*

"Curse it, Addy Louise, what are you doing to me?" he asked, sounding as helpless as she felt.

"The same thing you're doing to me, I expect."

He leaned his head down, pressing his forehead to hers. "You shouldn't be here."

"I excel at doing things I shouldn't do."

He chuckled, his breath falling on her lips in a hot little puff of air. "Of course you do."

She rubbed her nose against his, breathing deeply of his scent—shaving soap, citrus, a hint of musk. *Lion.*

And then Addy summoned her courage. "I came to you because I know that if I never see you again after I leave Marchingham Hall in the morning, I would forever regret not kissing you one last time."

A low sound came from deep in his throat, half groan, half growl. In the next instant, his lips covered hers. The kiss was devouring. Hungry and demanding. It was wild and unfettered. And then they were moving as one. Lion led her over the threshold. She was dimly aware of the sound of a door closing, of the light growing brighter around them.

They were in his bedroom.

*Alone.*

With the door closed and his mouth on hers.

If she had any sense of self-preservation, she would tear her lips from his and run. Mama had warned her many times against allowing gentlemen liberties. But running was the last thing on her mind. Because she was in Lion's room and his mouth was moving over hers and his hands were traveling over her body in a way that made her knees go weak. He was caressing her waist, her hips, his hands finding their way to her bottom.

His mouth left hers to run kisses along her jaw, to her ear. "I tried to resist you."

Lion's low, almost guttural admission had an instant effect upon her because she knew what it meant. He was surrendering.

She smiled, feeling a swell of triumph threading through the overwhelming desire. This cold, haughty, proper duke had finally given in to the potent magnetism between them. His fingers squeezed lightly, and he moved her body against his in a way that made her nipples tighten into aching points and the place between her legs grow restless with need.

Mama was also forever cautioning Addy against losing her virtue. But guarding it had been easy then. No suitor had ever tempted her. A few stolen kisses at a ball here or there had been the extent of her daring. Each time, she had been disappointed. Kisses were pleasant enough, but until she'd kissed Lion, she hadn't known they could be wondrous.

"What is it about you?" he muttered against her ear, sounding confounded.

She closed her eyes for a moment, savoring his nearness

and warmth, his body surrounding her, his hands on her. "I could ask you the same question."

"Why didn't you stay away?" He kissed the hollow behind her ear, eliciting a shiver from her.

She swallowed hard. "Because I couldn't."

She had asked herself the same question, agonizing over whether she should seek him out one last time or simply go safely to bed. She had paced her room until Dandy had been disturbed from slumber and had given her a halfhearted bark of protest. And in that moment, she had simply known.

Known it in her heart, in her marrow. She needed to take the chance. She'd tucked Dandy back into the coverlets and had left her bedroom, slipping through the shadows until she had found his door.

He dragged his nose along her temple, inhaling sharply. "Bloody hell."

She didn't think she had ever heard him curse before, and she knew she had never heard his voice so raw with emotion. His hands moved to her waist, and he gently pushed her from him without breaking his hold.

"If you stay here, I cannot promise to behave honorably," he said.

She slid her hands from his shoulders to his chest, his warmth searing her through the silk of his dressing gown. "I don't care."

"You should care. And I shouldn't be—"

She interrupted his attempts at swaying her from her course by pressing a finger to his lips. "Hush."

And then, holding his gaze, she took a step back, her hands going to the fastening of her dressing gown. He released her, his eyes darkening.

"Addy."

He said her name like a plea. She ignored him, intent upon her task. Despite Mama's firm determination to keep her woefully ignorant of what passed between a woman and a man, Addy had sought the answers. She knew what she was doing. Knew what she wanted and what she had to do.

Her fingers moved over buttons, the dressing gown opening to reveal her nightgown beneath. Lion watched, his expression turning ravenous, offering no further protestations. The air felt as if it were charged with a hidden electrical current. Addy reached the final mooring and then shrugged the garment from her shoulders. It fell softly to the carpet at her feet.

They stared at each other, not speaking a word, the silence saying more than either of them could. There was no sound, save the crackling of the fire in the grate and their ragged breathing.

Her mind was firmly made up in that moment. She was going to give herself to this man.

Addy caught the filmy fabric of her nightgown in both hands, and before her bravery could falter, she tugged it over her head, tossing it behind her. She stood there, completely bare in the chill night air, her body his to examine, his to touch, his to take.

For a long, heavy pause, he didn't move. His countenance may as well have been hewn in granite. His icy-blue stare traveled over her as she fought the urge to cover her breasts or shield her sex or—heaven forbid—race to pick up her discarded nightgown from the floor and pull it back over her head.

But then he moved with such sudden haste that she nearly jumped. Before she could even blink, Lion bent and scooped her into his arms with seemingly effortless ease. She clung to his neck as he carried her to his bed and tenderly placed her in the center of it, joining her there. He cupped her face and kissed her deeply.

Here was the answer she had been seeking.

Lion wasn't going to reject her.

His big body angled over hers, still clad in his dressing gown, their bare calves and ankles tangling as their lips moved as one. He kissed her slowly, sensuously, and then his touch moved lightly over her body, caressing her with increasing purpose as he grazed the edge of one bare breast. When he palmed it, the sensation struck her like lightning, starting where their bare skin connected and shooting through every part of her, all the way to her toes.

His thumb traced over her nipple, and she gasped into his kiss, her back arching. Lion groaned and plucked at the pebbled peak. His thigh pressed between her legs. Sensation blossomed, pleasure radiating outward from every place they touched.

Belatedly, it occurred to her how unfair it was for him to be fully clothed while she was naked. He was yet wearing his dressing gown, and her fingers itched to touch him. To feel the strength of his chest and the muscles of his back. To absorb his warmth and vitality. To stroke and caress him everywhere and learn each inch of his body, just as he was exploring hers.

She found the buttons on his dressing gown and somehow managed to slide a few free without breaking his kiss. But when her eager fingers found bare chest beneath, he lifted his head, his gaze searching hers, a question lingering there.

Addy understood what he was asking without words.

"I want to," she reassured him softly.

He shook his head slightly, as if trying to shake himself from a stupor. "You don't understand."

She kissed his chin and continued pulling buttons free. "I do."

She wasn't as experienced as he likely believed her to be, given her reputation and the scandals she'd caused on both sides of the Atlantic. But she knew enough to understand what it would mean to lie with him. To understand that she wanted it, despite the risks and consequences. After tonight, she would never have this chance again.

His dressing gown parted farther, and she found the sash at his waist, easily untangling the knot. She took advantage of the skin she had revealed, reveling in the play of the lamplight on his chest and upper arms, enjoying the smattering of gold hair that glinted on his chest, the way it teased her eager fingertips. How handsome and masculine and strong he was.

And how delightful she found the differences in their bodies, his broad chest and shoulders, his lean waist with its trail of hair leading down from his navel. He swallowed as she explored, leveraging himself on his forearms above her, his body rigid and tense. When she tried to reach lower, however, he kissed her again, temporarily staying her discovery.

His mouth was hot and firm, his tongue seeking entry. She opened for him, her hands slipping beneath the twain ends of his dressing gown so that she could glory in his bare chest. His heart thumped fast and hard against her palm. Almost impossible to believe she was naked in Marchingham's bed. Touching his bare skin. Helping him to disrobe.

The forbidden nature of their tryst only served to heighten her desire. Lying with him was wicked and wrong. They weren't married or engaged. Heavens, half the time, he disapproved of her so mightily that she thought she could drown in his disdain. But when he kissed her the way he was now, as if he could never have enough of her lips on his, nothing else mattered.

He caressed her breast again, the lightest of touches, and her sex clenched, the ache there deepening. She writhed against him, needing friction, needing him. He groaned into her mouth and then lifted his head to stare down at her as he played with her greedy nipple, and pangs of pure, sweet pleasure shot straight to her core.

"You're sure?"

She threaded her fingers through his hair, thinking him almost unbearably beautiful, his jaw angular and hard, his forehead high, his lips dark from the kisses they had shared, a lone golden wave falling rakishly over his brow. He kissed first her cheek, then her temple as he awaited her response.

Lion exhibited such tenderness that she could scarcely bear it. Something inside her cracked and fell open. Perhaps it was the walls she'd kept around her heart. Perhaps something even more fragile and sacred. All she knew was that she had fallen in love with Lion Hawthorne, Duke of Marchingham, a man who could never be hers beyond this night.

She lived in New York City.

His obligations and duties kept him here.

She was everything that horrified him.

He was all that repelled her.

Except, somehow along the course of her stay at Marchingham Hall, those sharp, distinct lines had blurred in immeasurable ways.

"I'm sure," she told him, meaning those words more than he could possibly know.

He hesitated, holding still above her, and for a heartbeat, she feared he had changed his mind. That his sense of honor had returned. But then he shifted, shrugging out of his dressing gown.

She helped him to remove it fully, drinking in every detail she could. His cock rose, ruddy and thick and proud between them. His naked body was a masterpiece. She kissed his neck, his shoulder, every part of him she could find, and when she flicked her tongue over his skin above the rigid protrusion of his collarbone, he tensed.

"What are you doing?"

"Tasting you," she admitted, savoring him on her tongue, salt and Lion.

He made a strangled sound. "My turn."

His head lowered again, but this time, he didn't kiss her. Instead, he took one of her nipples in his mouth and sucked.

"Oh," she gasped out, her toes curling into the cool bedclothes.

He took his time, sucking and licking, trailing lazy circles around the distended tip before doing the same to her other breast. Simultaneously, his hand came to her hip, caressing, tentative at first and then moving with greater purpose. His fingers traveled to her sex next, swirling over the sensitive bud hidden in her folds. She moved beneath him restlessly, seeking the pleasure of his touch. He seemed to know what she wanted, what she needed, drawing so deliciously on her nipples as he stroked over the swollen nub she only touched herself in the deepest depths of the night.

Doing so was a sin, she had been told in no uncertain terms at finishing school; each girl had been given a book explaining the evils of such a vulgar act. And yet, the release that came with it if she stroked herself enough and imagined it was someone else's hand on her had always made it worth the risk in Addy's opinion. The first time she had brought herself to her pinnacle, she had been terrified, so intense had been the previously unexperienced bliss. Not so terrified she hadn't done it again the next night, however.

Still, her own attempts to quell the need rising inside her were nothing compared to Lion's knowing hand on her, his fingers playing her as if she were an instrument and he alone could bring forth her music.

He released her nipple. "Do you like this, Addy?"

He was almost adorably concerned. Considerate and boyish, all the haughtiness he carried about like a shield conspicuously absent. He wasn't the duke but simply Lion, a man who wished to please her. A man with whom she longed to experience everything.

"Very much," she admitted, unashamed. "May I touch you?"

She was curious. Was he as sensitive as she was? Would he experience the same pleasure if she touched him? What would he feel like?

"Not yet," he denied when she reached for him, shifting his body slightly. "If you do, I'll never last."

She didn't know what that meant, didn't understand if it was good or bad. But she didn't want to admit to her lack of experience in congress between a man and woman, for fear that if she did, he would halt. She couldn't bear for him to stop. Not until it was over, and he was inside her.

She understood the mechanics of the act. She knew what her body wanted. It was the particular details that were lost upon her. She wanted Lion to teach her without realizing he was doing so.

So she turned herself over to him in body and mind. Banished her thoughts and simply allowed herself to feel. And oh, how she felt. She closed her eyes and savored his warmth, burning into her like the flames from the fire in the hearth. He increased the pressure over her as she wanted, until she was writhing, on the edge as he licked over her nipple then caught it between his teeth to gently nibble. She held her breath as the pleasure and the pressure heightened.

And then, suddenly, she splintered apart.

Addy cried out her pleasure to the ceiling, unable to contain herself.

Lion rose instantly, sealing his lips over hers and swallowing any further sounds she made. As he kissed her, he shifted yet again, and she knew a different sensation altogether. The thick, firm tip of his cock pressed against her, seeking entrance just where she wanted him.

He guided her legs around his hips and slicked himself up and down her folds as pleasure continued to ripple through her. She was open to him completely, their lower bodies perfectly aligned. He grasped himself and the pressure increased. She felt herself stretching around him, taking him in. Slowly, slowly, he eased deeper. There was a sharp twinge of pain, taking her by surprise. She stiffened and he stopped, tearing his mouth from hers to stare down at her.

"You're a virgin?" he asked, brow furrowed, the cords in his neck tensed and strained, as if he scarcely held himself in check.

Clearly, he had believed her not to be one. She refused to allow herself to feel anything about that realization just now. No, she would think about it later. For now, she would allow nothing and no one to ruin this moment and keep her from what she wanted.

Including Lion.

"Yes." Addy undulated her hips, trying to urge him on.

"Addy." His lips were set at a stubborn angle she recognized too well.

She didn't want to hear him prattling on about honor. So, she kissed him, openmouthed and unabashed, giving him her tongue. It was all the spurring he required. With a groan, he kissed her back, his tongue sliding against hers while thrusting into her. She knew another exacting pinch as her body adjusted to the unfamiliar invasion. He felt impossibly large and insistent, almost as if he would split her in two.

She held her breath, keeping still, tensing.

"I'm sorry," he murmured against her lips.

She didn't want his apologies. Didn't want his regrets.

"I'm not," she returned, arching her back and tentatively moving against him, following her body's instinctive urging. The slick glide of his shaft inside her elicited a new sensation. She felt gloriously full, wrapped in the warm strength of his big body atop her, within her.

With a groan, he kissed her harder, as if the last of his control had frayed and snapped. His hips canted into hers, driving him deeper and then withdrawing, his pace maddeningly slow. The pain was receding now to nothing more than a pang of discomfort. With each stroke, new pleasure shot through her, beginning at her center and radiating outward.

Addy touched him everywhere she could, trying to commit the lines of his body to memory so that even when she was at home in New York City, with an ocean between them, she could close her eyes and remember this night, the way he brought her to life. Her fingertips trailed over the taut blades of his shoulders, the muscles of his back and forearms, lingered in his silky gold waves. Touching him was a luxury, and she would miss it just as she would miss him.

But there was no thought for sadness now. No space for anything but the two of them, their bodies working together in ancient rhythm, pleasure sparking like dry kindling turning into roaring flame. He began thrusting inside her faster, harder, penetrating her deeply, losing his gentlemanly restraint. He no longer kissed her and made love to her as if she were fragile and delicate, and she was glad for it. She liked him this way, wild and untamed, all his elegant hauteur shattered.

He tore his mouth from hers, groaning her name. Bracing himself on one arm, he reached between them with his free hand, to where their bodies were joined. His fingers found her, stroking and teasing her needy flesh.

The ever-growing knot of pleasure tightened, heightened by each glide of him inside her. He took the peak of one breast into his mouth, and the hot suction sent her over the edge. She shuddered and clamped down on him, her body spasming around his thick length. Sparks skittered up and down her spine, and a rush so potent and unlike anything she'd ever known roared through her. All she could do was clutch him tightly and surrender to the fury of her release.

Lion continued, gliding in and out of her wetness, clutching her hip, making low sounds of helpless pleasure. Another few strokes, and he tensed, withdrawing from her so swiftly that she mourned the loss of him within her. Looming over her, he gripped himself. His expression awash with ecstasy, he painted her inner thigh with his seed before collapsing to the bed at her side, his breathing as ragged as hers.

# CHAPTER 8

Recriminations swirled through Lion as he lay by Addy's side in his bed, naked and spent, his heart pounding and his mind in ruins.

She had been a virgin. He'd been so caught up in her that he hadn't given a thought to her experience other than those supposed kisses from the Swiss lads. But when she had held his gaze and lifted her nightgown over her head, revealing her lush curves and gorgeous body, he had lost his ability to control himself. Had he been as gentle as he should have been? Had he taken his time and eased her into lovemaking?

He hadn't been a virgin in what felt like a lifetime. His first lover had been an experienced widow who had tutored him well in the art of pleasing a woman. Had he ever made love to a virgin? He didn't think he had.

*Dear God.* He had taken Miss Adelia Fox's maidenhead.

Had spent on her thigh little better than a mongrel in heat. What a beast he was.

He was going to have to marry her, and for reasons he could not presently comprehend, the notion of taking Addy as his wife didn't bother him nearly as much as it should. In fact, it didn't bother him at all. Quite the opposite.

He *wanted* to marry her.

This astounding realization struck him like a blow.

Swallowing hard against a rush of emotion, he turned to find her watching him, her lips swollen from his kisses. Her eyes seemed even more vibrantly green in the low light. Her nipples were hard, pink points, jutting toward him in invitation. Her hair was a burnished cloud on his pillow. She looked at home in his bed, as if she belonged there. He'd never had a woman in his bed here at Marchingham Hall, and the astounding rightness of her presence made his chest tighten.

That was when his gaze traveled lower, finding the reminder of what they had just done together.

His seed was on her thigh.

"Are you…" His words trailed off haltingly as he fought to regain his composure. Lion cleared his throat and tried anew. "Did I hurt you?"

"A bit of pain is to be expected a woman's first time," she said softly, indirectly answering his question.

He *had* hurt her. Ballocks.

"I'm sorry."

"That is the second time you've said so."

She sounded cross.

"Addy," he tried, not knowing what to say or how to ameliorate the damage of what he had just done.

The edicts of his father had made an indelible mark upon him. He had taken great care to avoid scandal at all costs. Deflowering a hoyden American heiress in his own bed was the decided opposite of that.

"What are you sorry for?" she asked sharply.

"For hurting you. For behaving dishonorably. For taking unacceptable liberties. For…everything."

"Everything?"

Her voice was as taut as a wire pulled to its tightest, just before breaking.

He was making a mess of this.

"Yes. I never intended for this to happen between us." But the moment she had appeared at his door, a sensual goddess he could not resist, it had been inevitable.

"And you regret it."

"Of course I do." Because it was wrong, what he had done. A gentleman should never take a lady's innocence. Not without the sanctity of marriage.

"Lowering yourself to touching a dreadful Yankee is undoubtedly distasteful," she said, sitting up.

Christ.

He sat up as well.

"My regret has nothing to do with the fact that you are an American," he denied, placing a gentle hand on her arm. "Let me attend you."

"Attend me? I should think you've already done enough of that." There was a smirk on her lips, but Addy didn't fool him. He knew her well enough to see the cracks in her façade. Her bravado was a mask she wore to fool the world.

He kissed her firmly but gently, then cupped her cheek, holding her gaze. "Don't move."

Although he was reasonably certain all the bones in his body had melted in the wake of the intense passion they'd just shared, he rose from the bed and crossed the room, seeking the wash basin. He felt her stare on his naked arse all the while, and he wondered what she was thinking as he wetted a cloth and wrung it out. He was more than aware that the finer sex found him attractive. He reveled in the outdoors, in tending things on the estate, in rowing and riding. His body was well honed and muscular, and the women in his bed had never found fault with it.

But still, this was Addy, and she was different.

He couldn't describe how. It was simply so.

Lion turned back to find her sitting where he had left her, countenance inscrutable. At least she had obeyed him, but he wasn't fool enough to comment upon it, lest she dash from his bedroom entirely nude just to be contrary.

He moved back to the bed.

She stiffened. "What are you doing?"

"Tending to you."

Her chin went up. "I am adept at tending to myself."

He heard the pride in her voice. Stubborn wench.

Lion met her gaze. "I do not doubt it. But in this instance, I hope you will allow me to clean the mess I've made."

It was the only polite way he could think of referring to the white lashings of his mettle on her thigh. His gaze dipped to the evidence of what they had done, and his cock twitched. He didn't think he'd ever seen a more erotic sight than his mark upon her creamy skin. It made him want her again, even if his rational mind knew that could not happen.

"Very well," she allowed, her voice husky.

He took the damp cloth and wiped his seed from her, almost hating to remove it. A possessive surge took hold in him. This lovely, brazen, unique woman so unlike any he had ever known was his now.

All he had to do was offer for her.

But would she accept?

Lion wanted to ask her. All he had to do was summon the proper means of doing so. Hovering over her, naked and bearing a cloth coated in his mettle, after he had just taken her maidenhead outside the bonds of matrimony, was hardly good form.

He finished his task, painfully aware of her proximity, her nudity, her gaze on him. She was lying there, her glorious body gilded by the lamplight, making no effort to shield herself, and he was the world's greatest oaf, because all he could think about was joining her on the bed and making love to her a second time.

"There we are," he said, his voice thick.

"Thank you." Her voice was a husky murmur, reminding him of the sounds she had made when she had come undone.

Clearing his throat, he turned away from the tantalizing sight she presented and returned the cloth to the washstand. "You needn't thank me. Given my conduct, it's hardly warranted."

"But I liked your conduct."

He closed his eyes and bowed his head, willing his thickening cock to go limp. He must not give in to temptation a second time.

Lion swallowed. He was no longer a randy lad, ready for bed sport to begin anew a few minutes after he'd reached completion. And yet, there was no denying the rekindling desire burning hot within him. He was dangerously near to making love to Addy a second time. And that wouldn't do. He needed to get the both of them dressed and see her back to her room.

"We should dress," he forced out, cursing himself for the coldness in his voice.

He hadn't intended to be so curt with her.

"Of course," she said, her voice sounding suddenly small. "I suppose you'll want your bed back now, and I should return to my room so that no one else discovers our sordid little secret."

He was going about this all wrong. Lion winced as he spun back to find her hastening from his bed.

"You are not my sordid little secret," he denied, even as he realized that was precisely how she believed he was treating her.

But damnation, what was he meant to do? He was

attempting to preserve her reputation and go about this the right way. He wasn't in the business of despoiling virgins. He hadn't an inkling of what to do in the aftermath.

As he wrestled with himself, Addy found her nightgown and drew it over her head. He mourned the loss of her silken curves, all sweet cream and palest pink. And then he recalled that he needed to don his dressing gown. Angling his body away from hers so that she wouldn't spy his rapidly hardening cock, he stalked across the faded Axminster and seized his discarded dressing gown, drawing it on. His fingers fumbled over buttons.

"You needn't deny it," Addy was saying. "You won't hurt my feelings. I've always known you disapprove of me, and coming to your room tonight was reckless and rash. I'm sure it didn't help your poor opinion. You hardly want your faultless reputation besmirched because of me."

He faltered on the fastenings of his robe. What must she think of him? That he would bed her while disdaining her?

"I don't have a poor opinion of you, Addy," he told her. "And I don't give a damn about my reputation."

"Ha! Don't lie to me, please. I may be many things, but I'm no fool." She stuffed her arms into the sleeves of her dressing gown. "I came to you because I wanted to experience what it's like between a man and a woman, and now I have. I thank you for the lesson. It proved quite…insightful."

"Addy," he protested, realizing he had done up his buttons all wrong. "I'm not lying to you."

Blast. He couldn't go about the halls in *dishabille*. If a servant were to come upon them or, God forbid, the elder Miss Fox, he shuddered to think what would happen. He began undoing the buttons with the intention of setting them to rights, but she was flitting to the door, already clothed.

"Good night, Lion."

Her expression, like her voice, was lamenting.

Bloody hell, his erection had finally begun to subside thanks to their argument, but his dressing gown was gaping open, his cock jutting in the wind. He couldn't chase after her like this.

"Don't go," he bit out.

Not yet. Not like this. He wanted—strike that, he *needed*—to explain himself. To make this right. But Addy ignored him, flouncing out of his bedroom and closing the door at her back.

Lion puffed out a weary sigh and ran a hand through his hair. Somehow, he had taken the most incredible night of his life and tossed it away into the dustbin. For a moment, he considered rushing after her, but he thought better of it. By the time he was able to properly fasten his dressing gown, she would likely be tucked away in her own chamber. He could scarcely break the door down and ask her to marry him.

No, he would wait until the morning and explain himself.

Everything would be right then.

Feeling weary and yet deeply content in a way he'd never known, Lion undressed and turned down the lamps before slipping into a bed that smelled of violets and orris root and the woman he intended to make his duchess.

Slumber claimed him with ease.

Ever since her mad dash from Lion's room in the midst of the night, Addy hadn't been able to sleep. The hour was pitifully early, but she was up anyway, dressed for travel and determined to pretend as if she hadn't gone to his chamber, taken off all her clothes, and given him her virginity.

It was a feat that would be easier said than accomplished, she knew.

She could still feel Lion's hands on her, his lips on her body, his mouth on her breasts, could still feel him moving inside her. She knew a few twinges of soreness between her legs as she made her way down the grand staircase.

Making love with him had been nothing short of life-altering for her. She would never be the same.

What had come after had been…well, mortifying. He had reverted to his proper self, growing cold and ducal. Telling her he regretted what had happened. The latter had been akin to a knife in her heart. The heart that he unwittingly owned.

It was best that she and Aunt Pearl were leaving today. They could make it to York and take the train to London, celebrating Christmas at a hotel. Addy would simply do her utmost to pretend as if the Duke of Marchingham didn't exist.

Which would be nothing short of impossible.

She sighed as she reached the last step, not regretting that she had been reckless enough to go to Lion last night, but rather, wishing that their time together had ended differently. As she made her way toward the breakfast room, a sudden flurry of activity caught her attention. It sounded as if it were coming from the great hall—a chorus of voices, two of which were feminine and familiar.

Her breath hitched. Letty and Lila? Surely it couldn't be. They were spending Christmas with their aunt and uncle. The roads had only just become passable after the snowstorm. And yet…

Her feet flew with a mind of their own, taking her to the great hall, where Lion's deep baritone cut through the chorus of voices.

"Violetta and Lila," he greeted warmly. "It is good to see you again, sisters."

Addy stopped at the periphery of the great hall, where antlers and familial busts lingered in the shadows. Two young ladies stood with Lion, dressed in travel garments and grinning widely, one red-haired and the other possessing white-gold hair even lighter than Lion's.

Letty and Lila were here at Marchingham Hall. Behind them, an older, distinguished-looking couple stood, also dressed for travel. Presumably, they were the aunt and uncle.

A thrill rose within her at the sight of her beloved friends. She longed to rush to them, to embrace them, and yet, she was painfully aware of Lion's presence. His back was to her, and he had no notion of her presence. She wasn't certain she could bear to look at him by morning light without expiring from mortification.

What must he think of her?

Did he truly regret what had happened?

She had known there would be consequences. Addy took a deep breath, deciding that she must face them. Her boldness had always stood her in good stead. She wouldn't allow it to fail her now.

"Letty," she exclaimed warmly, bustling forward, a smile fixed on her lips as she avoided looking at Lion. "Lila!"

Her friends looked at her in unison, their surprise evident as their eyes lit up and their mouths fell open.

"Addy!" Letty was the first to react, grinning as she rushed toward her and folded Addy in an embrace. "You're here at Marchingham Hall!"

Smiling, Addy returned her friend's exuberant hug. "So are you."

Lila was swift to join them, throwing her arms around them both. They rejoiced, talking over top of one another, their years of separation falling away. It was instantly like their finishing school days.

"What are you doing in Yorkshire?" Letty asked.

Her friend's question made Addy painfully aware of Lion's solemn regard. Of all that had transpired since her arrival. Heat crept up her throat and over her cheeks. Surely her friends didn't suspect that she had fallen in love with their brother. Nor that she had spent a goodly portion of last night in his bed. Her guilt wouldn't be written across her face, would it?

"Addy?" Lila pressed, eagerly awaiting her response, no doubt.

She cleared her throat. "I thought to surprise the both of you. Since you weren't able to join me for Christmas, I decided to come to you here in Yorkshire. Unfortunately, neither of you was in residence."

"When did you arrive?" Lila asked.

"Eleven days ago."

"Eleven days?"

"During a snowstorm," she elaborated.

"You've been stranded here at Marchingham Hall all this time?" Letty shook her head. "You poor darling. You must have been terribly bored with nothing except our brother and his disapproving glares for company."

He didn't always give her disapproving glares. No indeed, sometimes he looked at her with the blazing intensity of the sun, and she could do nothing but bask in it even if she knew there was a strong chance she would be relentlessly burned. She was Icarus, flying too close to the sun. Only, the sea she had drowned in had been Lion himself.

"I had Aunt Pearl," she said weakly, studiously avoiding Lion's gaze.

"Your aunt Pearl has accompanied you? Oh, we must

meet her!" Letty exclaimed, clapping excitedly. "We've heard so very much about her from your letters."

"And you must meet our aunt and uncle, Lord and Lady Hargrove," Lila added. "How utterly thrilling this is. We thought to surprise Lion for Christmas, but the roads were covered in snow and we had to wait a few days in York. I had feared we would be stranded in a hotel until the roads finally became passable. But we had no notion you were here as well."

What could she say to that? Her smile felt as if it had been pinned in place by an enterprising seamstress, and the heat in her cheeks continued to prickle. It didn't help that Lion still watched her, silent and unsmiling.

What was he thinking? Were his regrets even stronger this morning than they had been last night? A maelstrom of emotions had whipped up within her. She had been ready to flee before descending the staircase. But now her friends were here, at last. They were smiling and overjoyed to see her, and she felt the same way. There remained, however, the cloud of what had happened between herself and their brother hanging overhead.

Letty and Lila must never know, she decided in that moment.

"I am so happy to see you both," she said. "Aunt Pearl and I are set to leave this morning. Had you been any later in your arrival, I would have missed you."

"Surely you will alter your plans now," Lila said.

"Of course she will." Letty turned to Lion. "Addy must stay now that we've arrived, don't you agree, brother?"

Addy dared to glance in his direction now. His icy-blue gaze clashed with hers, sending a jolt of awareness through her. How she wished she could read what lay within those blue depths.

He inclined his head, his countenance remaining as

forbidding as ever. "Naturally, Miss Fox is welcome at Marchingham Hall. She may stay for as long as she likes."

*Forever*, some raw, ridiculous voice cried out inside her. A voice Addy promptly stifled. Lion may have given in to their mutual attraction, but the aftermath of their lovemaking last night had made it abundantly clear to her that his poor opinion of her had not changed.

She swallowed hard, ignoring her stinging pride and aching heart. "That is most generous of you, Your Grace."

"It's settled!" Letty announced. "You'll stay for Christmas."

"But—" Addy began to protest.

"Nonsense," Lila interrupted. "We've only just been reunited. *Les Trois Mousquetaires* must have the proper time to chat after all these years apart. Letters are woefully insufficient, do you not find?"

"I—" Addy started, only to be cut short yet again, this time by Letty.

"Of course she does, and that is why she is here. Come, let us introduce you to our aunt and uncle."

Addy was scarcely aware of the introductions that were performed. Lord Hargrove was a stern-faced, elegant gentleman with silver hair and a neatly trimmed mustache. Lady Hargrove bore an obvious resemblance to Lila, Letty, and Lion, her golden hair shot through with threads of gray and white, her eyes the same icy blue. Her astute gaze traveled between Addy and Lion as conversation whirled about, her expression ever so slightly calculating.

Aunt Pearl arrived and a second round of introductions unfolded, and as portmanteaus were brought in by footmen, it was decided that everyone would convene for breakfast. Addy and Aunt Pearl's departure was temporarily delayed. As Addy was led off by her eagerly chattering friends, she told herself that she could withstand a few more days at Marchingham Hall.

She would simply keep her distance from Lion, enjoy spending time with Letty and Lila, and forget last night had ever happened.

*Impossible*, whispered that same, taunting voice within her.

It was a voice Addy was determined to ignore.

# CHAPTER 9

As he had so frequently over the last thirteen days, Lion was once again hiding in his study. But no amount of poring over ledgers, reports, and correspondence could sufficiently distract him.

Two days filled with his sisters, aunt and uncle, Addy, and her aunt Pearl had proven rather akin to a boiling pot that was rapidly overflowing, making a mess of everything. Too many voices, too much excitement. Too many people suddenly descending upon his household when he had arisen that morning with the intention of asking Addy for her hand in marriage and righting the wrongs he had committed when he had taken her virginity.

Uncle Algernon had his ear for much of the two days since their arrival, droning on about horseflesh and bloodlines and a mare he had his eye on, along with everything from his gout to his older brother's biliousness. Aunt Helene's shrewd gaze had taken in the tension between Lion and Addy even as his sisters had failed to yet take note. Letty and Lila had been too busy laughing and prattling about everything from their finishing school scrapes to Worth gowns to New York City and London gossip.

*Letty?*

He frowned down at the assortment of papers he was ignoring on his desk. Since when had he begun to think of his own sister, whom he had known all her life, as Letty? Addy had not just managed to find her way into his bed, but into his mind as well. And, if he were honest, perhaps into another part of himself as well.

His heart.

Lion exhaled a puff of air, wishing he had a cigar or even a glass of port with which he might sufficiently distract himself. This was madness. He couldn't hide in his study forever. He would have to emerge and somehow separate Addy from his sisters' clutches so that he could have a private word with her. Two days had passed. Christmas was on the morrow. And he had yet to have a moment alone with her, let alone an audience in which he could ask for her hand.

A tapping at his door broke through his thoughts. Lion rose, hoping it was Addy. Perhaps she was as eager to find time with him as he was with her. Perhaps she had finally surrendered and stolen away from his sisters' sides.

"Come," he called.

But it wasn't Addy's golden hair and dancing green eyes that greeted him when the portal opened. Rather, it was his father's youngest sister. Aunt Helene had not been cut from the same cruel cloth as Lion's sire, but she was a cunning woman. He had no wish to be interrogated by her at the moment.

Still, he bowed. "Aunt Helene."

"Marchingham." She left the door ajar as she swept into the room, wearing a handsome gown of lavender silk. "I was wondering if I might speak with you."

*Blast.*

"Of course." He gestured to the armchairs flanking the hearth. "Would you care to sit?"

She crossed the room toward the seating area, and they both sat. His aunt regarded him for a moment.

"It is good to see you again, Marchingham," she said. "When your sisters suggested traveling to you for Christmas, I will admit that I was hesitant to do so because I know how you prefer your solitude."

He did like solitude. Or, rather, he *had* liked being alone. Now...well, the boisterous Addy Fox had changed him, and he couldn't deny it.

"I'm pleased to have company, particularly for Christmas." As the words left him, Lion realized they were truth rather than a polite platitude.

He had not celebrated Yuletide in years, not since his mother had been alive. In opposition to his father, each year, she had overseen the hanging of kissing balls and fir boughs and even erected a tree in the drawing room that had been ringed with gifts. His sire had deemed the festivities unnecessary folderol and had preferred to stay in London. After his mother had died, Lion hadn't had the heart to continue her traditions. Instead, he had sent his sisters away and remained within the seclusion of Marchingham Hall, busying himself with estate matters and attending his duties.

"I always believed you were in my brother's mold in regard to Christmas gaiety," Aunt Helene observed.

"I have no wish to be in his mold," he answered with raw honesty. "Not in any way."

"He was a harsh man," Aunt Helene agreed, giving Lion a pitying look that made him want to writhe in his chair. "It has always aggrieved me to know how cold he was to you and your sisters, how unfeeling."

He was not comfortable speaking about his sire and rarely did so, which was why he had been so startled when he had revealed so much to Addy about Mittens. She simply had a way with him. She didn't dismantle his walls; she galloped past them and turned them into dust.

"It is in the past now," he managed. "You are not responsible for your brother's faults."

"Quite a mercy, that," Aunt Helene responded wryly. "My brother had many, many faults. He was far too much like our father and not nearly enough like our mother. *Maman* was an angel amongst mere mortals. I shall never know what she saw in Father, but whatever it was, he worked diligently for the entirety of their marriage to destroy it."

Lion knew that his grandfather had been a wastrel and a faithless rake; he had died of apoplexy just before Lion had been born, so he'd never known him. The conquests of the sixth Duke of Marchingham, however, had been much written and whispered about. Lion was also well aware that Aunt Helene had not come to his study to relive past disappointments.

"I cannot think you sought me out to speak about my grandfather's shortcomings," he said.

"Quite right," she drawled. "Otherwise, we would still be speaking well into next year. The reason I wished to speak with you is decidedly different. It concerns Miss Fox."

The mere mentioning of Addy was enough to make his blood heat. Although he had made a colossal mess by bedding her and failing to ask her to marry him in that moment, he wanted her more than ever. Each hour that passed whilst she merrily avoided him in favor of his sisters was utter torture. If he didn't soon get her alone, he would go mad.

"What of Miss Fox?" he asked, struggling to keep his voice neutral.

"I've seen the way you look at her," Aunt Helene said.

Lion's spine stiffened. "I have no notion what you're speaking about."

"I think you do."

Curse Aunt Helene. She knew him too well. Years ago, she and Uncle Algernon had stepped into a maternal and paternal role for not just Letty and Lila, but Lion as well.

He sighed. "I intend to ask Miss Fox to marry me."

"That is wonderful news." Aunt Helene pressed a hand over her heart. "Your uncle and I have been fretting over the state of Marchingham Hall and your other estates. My brother left you heavily in debt. Miss Fox is a wealthy heiress in her own right. Marrying her shall solve all your financial problems. An American heiress is precisely what you need."

His aunt and uncle had repeatedly offered to loan him the necessary funds, but Lion had been too proud. He was determined to do what he could on his own. Marrying Addy would change that, but he would have to swallow his pride where she was concerned. She was accustomed to a lavish life in New York City, and he would not expect her to suffer here.

"Yes," he agreed reluctantly. "It will."

He kept the rest of what he might have said to himself. This was the first he had even contemplated Addy's fortune. He was aware she was an heiress; that much was impossible to ignore. But it hadn't been the promise of her wealth enabling him to pay off his looming debts that had drawn him to her. Rather, it had been Addy herself.

"You'll no longer have to sell off any of the estates," Aunt Helene added. "Marchingham Hall has been in desperate need of a restoration since I was a girl, and that was many years ago now."

"It is long past time that the leaking roof is repaired and the threadbare Axminster is taken away," he agreed.

"You will want to hire additional domestics as well, I

should think. How you have managed to carry on here with scarcely any maids and footmen is beyond my ken. Do you even have a head gardener?"

"Mr. Morton left three years ago." He frowned, thinking. "Or perhaps it was four."

Aunt Helene shuddered. "I thought the rosebushes looked snarled. And the boxwoods, my dear boy. They are woefully in wont of trimming. Then, there is the matter of the stables. Your uncle was horrified by your lack of horseflesh. My father had a fine head for the equine. Indeed, it was perhaps the only thing at which he excelled, unless one counts gambling, drinking to excess, and taking mistresses. I suppose you've had to sell off all the finest mounts in an effort to keep the creditors away."

A sound at the study door—the telltale creak of a floorboard—caught Lion's attention then. He glanced toward the hall but didn't see anyone. More than likely, it had been one of the servants. Dismissing it, he turned back to the conversation at hand.

Aunt Helene was ordinarily far too mild-mannered to dare to speak of scandalous moral failings or—God forbid—money aloud. He wondered if she had made her way into the wine cellar after breakfast. Her fondness for good French wine was no secret, and the well-preserved bottles at Marchingham Hall were one of few assets that had not been depleted, gambled away, or sold off by the previous Dukes of Marchingham.

Discreetly, he gave the air a sniff, but he didn't detect the familiar scent. "We have had to sell many of the Highland ponies, Arabians, and Clydesdales, along with some Gainsborough landscapes, two Titians, and a Rembrandt."

"The Titians?" Aunt Helene held a hand to her brow at the news. "Why did you not tell me, nephew? Your uncle would have been more than happy to—"

"Because I'll not accept charity," he interrupted gently. "You know that, Aunt Helene. I am indebted to you and Uncle Algernon for the generosity of heart and spirit you have shown my sisters and me over the years, but I cannot accept anything else from you. To do so would be a shameful breach."

Aunt Helene and Uncle Algernon had no living children of their own, but they had taken Lion and his sisters under their collective wing. He would sooner eat his boot than presume upon their relationship. The paintings had fetched handsome sums from wealthy collectors in their own right.

"At least securing an alliance with a wealthy heiress will keep you from having to sell any of the others," Aunt Helene said mournfully.

He loved his aunt dearly, but Lion did not care for the way she was framing his impending nuptials to Addy.

"You should know that Miss Fox's fortune is not the reason I intend to ask for her hand," he cautioned. "Over the course of her stay here, I have become quite fond of her."

"Quite fond?" Aunt Helene prodded slyly.

He sighed. "I have fallen in love with her, if you must know."

There. He had said it aloud. The sentiment that had been growing inside him, at first a small seed that had taken root and burst into a full bloom, would not be contained. Nor could he continue to pretend as if his heart didn't beat for the most maddening woman he had ever known.

"You're in love with Miss Fox," Aunt Helene repeated, her smile blinding.

He shook his head. "I couldn't explain it if I tried. We are opposites in so many ways—she is sunshine to my darkness, the summer to my winter, loud when I am quiet, bold and brazen and stubborn and determined and intelligent and ridiculous and...*right* for me. Somehow, in a way I cannot begin to comprehend, she is right for me." He paused, sighing. "All I need to do is convince her to marry me."

"That should be easy," Aunt Helene reassured him. "You are the Duke of Marchingham. Any lady in England would be thrilled to take her place."

Her confidence in him pleased Lion. But if she had only witnessed the debacle he had made with Addy several nights before, he had no doubt that her opinion might have been a different one. Still, he could hardly explain to his aunt that he had deflowered Addy in his bed then hopelessly mangled his attempt at offering for her.

So he gave her a tight smile instead. "Thank you, Aunt Helene. Your faith in me is greatly appreciated."

He could only hope that her belief was not misplaced.

Addy hastened to her room, her eyes so blurred by tears she could scarcely find her way through the sprawling manor house. Somehow, she managed to make it to the private sanctity of the chamber, closing the door at her back before she began to weep.

Dandy, who had been sleeping on the bed, leapt off at once and raced to her with a little bark as if to ask what was wrong. Sniffling, Addy bent down to pat her beloved companion's silken head.

"Oh, Dandy," she whispered. "*Everything* is wrong."

Dandy licked her hand, offering comfort.

What a fool she was.

She had fallen in love with a man who not only didn't return her feelings, but who wanted to marry her only for the fortune she could bring him. Two whole days of holding her head high, pretending as if her heart didn't beat for him, as if her breath didn't catch and heat didn't lick through her veins each time she inhabited the same room as him. Two days of waiting and hoping that he might approach her and give her a reason to stay on at Marchingham Hall after Christmas. And in the end, she had learned of his intention to propose marriage in the cruelest possible way.

With a sob, Addy marched to the linen press as Dandy trailed after her, throwing it open and unceremoniously hauling all the garments that had been placed within yet again after she and Aunt Pearl had decided to stay on at Marchingham Hall for Christmas.

There was no chance of that now.

She could not possibly bear to remain beneath the same roof as Marchingham for another night. She would have to give Letty and Lila their gifts before she went. Addy dashed at the scalding tears on her cheeks with the back of her hand.

Lady Hargrove's voice had carried to Addy when she had innocently approached his study door, intending to have an audience with him after being unable to find him alone for the past two days.

*Marrying her shall solve all your financial problems.*

Addy had halted at the threshold, wondering if Lion had a betrothed and he had neglected to inform her.

Then his voice had come, deep and sure.

*Yes. It will.*

*An American heiress is precisely what you need*, Lady Hargrove had said.

Addy's heart had fallen, her chest seizing as she'd realized they were speaking about her. That Lion, the man who had kissed her so ardently, touched her so reverently, had only done so because of who she was and not because he had wanted *her*.

Everything had been a lie.

*It is long past time that the leaking roof is repaired and the threadbare Axminster is taken away*, he had said conversationally, as if he and his aunt were discussing nothing of greater significance than what was to be had for breakfast in the morning.

Meanwhile, her heart had been quietly shattering into a thousand pieces.

Lady Hargrove had carried on in her no-nonsense fashion while Addy's stomach had churned, making a list of all the repairs that could be made and the new servants to be brought on. Addy hadn't been able to bear another second. She had rushed away, not caring if anyone heard or saw her. Not caring about anyone or anything, trapped in the vicious maw of betrayal.

She ought to have known.

She was no stranger to fortune hunters.

All around her had been the signs that Marchingham Hall was failing, that Lion was in desperate need of funds. Threadbare carpet, missing pictures, few servants, simple fare at the table, overgrown gardens. Letty and Lila themselves had recently been lamenting the lack of pin money their brother had granted them, of the necessity for reworking their gowns from previous seasons so that they weren't outmoded.

And what had Addy done? She had served herself to him on a silver platter, chasing after him like a brazen strumpet. Giving herself to him.

Had his lovemaking been a lie as well?

Dear God, how utterly mortifying.

Another sob tore from her. Dandy pawed at her skirts and whined, agitated by Addy's distress. Addy bent and scooped up her beloved little dog. Dandy promptly licked her cheek, cleaning her tears.

Addy Fox was the world's greatest idiot. But somehow, she had discovered the Duke of Marchingham's game before it was too late.

She knew what she had to do.

"You're leaving?" Lila asked, incredulous.

"The day before Christmas?" Letty added, aghast. "But Addy, you simply can't. We've only just arrived."

They had gathered around the hearth in Lila's bedroom, which had become their meeting place of the past few days. Lila's room was more spacious and had three chairs drawn round the cozy fireplace, along with windows that received a great deal of sunshine.

"I'm afraid I must," Addy said, struggling to maintain her flagging composure. "My father sent word from New York City that I am to return home at once."

It was a convenient falsehood.

She'd received no such summons. But lying to her friends felt so much easier than confessing the sordid truth, which was that she had thrown herself at their brother, given herself to him, and had subsequently discovered he intended to marry her to save his estate from ruin. Not because he cared for her. Not because he couldn't bear to live without her.

No, because she was an heiress, and like so many impoverished aristocrats, Lion needed the lifeblood of her dowry to revive his dying ancestral lands. Had he been relieved when she had arrived at his bedroom that night? Or had he been horrified by her lack of propriety? Likely, a blend of both.

To her everlasting humiliation, she would never know the answer for certain.

"Has something happened?" Lila queried.

Addy's cheeks went hot, guilt making her spine straighten. "Of course not. Why would you ask such a thing?"

"Because your father has summoned you home," Lila explained. "Surely there would be a reason for it. He knew you intended to spend Christmas here, did he not?"

She blinked. Lila was not speaking about Lion. Of course she hadn't been.

"All is well," she managed shakily. "My father…misses me. And so does my fiancé."

The moment the lie emerged from her, Addy wished she could recall it. Likely, it was her wounded pride and her guilty conscience mingling together, making her blurt nonsense. But she needed a reason to retreat to York at once. And inventing a fiancé seemed a reasonable enough one.

"You're betrothed?" Lila and Letty demanded as one.

"Why didn't you say so before now?" Letty demanded.

"You never spoke a word about an engagement in any of your letters," Lila added.

Addy licked her lips. "It was meant to be a secret. We aren't going to announce it until our engagement ball. But my fiancé has…fallen from a horse and broken his leg. I'll need to return and help tend to him."

"Good heavens, he's broken his leg?" Letty shook her head. "How dreadful. Of course you must return to him."

"What is his name?" Lila asked.

*Drat.*

"George," she blurted. "Mr. George…Smith."

"I've never heard of the Smiths from New York," Lila said. "Is he from a good family?"

Addy's stomach swirled. "Yes, of course."

"Are you in love?" Letty demanded.

She thought of Lion and closed her eyes for a moment, struggling to keep her tears at bay. "I am, yes."

Lila was looking at her closely when she opened them again, her regard intent. "Why didn't you tell us before now?

You must know we would guard your secrets with our very lives."

"I've had such a wonderful time with you both that it slipped my mind," she said.

Only half of that statement was a lie. She *had* enjoyed visiting with her dearest friends. For two extraordinary days, it had been as if no time had passed since they had parted ways at the Académie Clairemont.

"We've had a marvelous time with you as well," Lila said, laying a hand on Addy's arm. "I hate for you to leave so soon. If we had known you were here…"

"It is my own foolish fault for trying to surprise you without making certain you would be at Marchingham Hall," Addy reassured her friend, guilt still curdling her stomach. "But it would be remiss for me to leave without giving you your Christmas gifts first."

She scooped up the small parcels she had brought with her from New York City and offered one to each sister.

"Gifts! But we haven't a gift for you," Letty protested.

There was only one gift Addy wanted, and it was the gift of having her broken heart healed. But she couldn't say that. It was imperative that she forget all about Lion. If she told her friends what had happened, they would likely be angry with their brother on her behalf, and she couldn't bring herself to be the cause of a familial rift. The three siblings needed one another.

"Nonsense," she said, forcing a smile. "Open them, if you please."

Her friends did so in unison, each one gasping as she lifted the earrings from their box. Sapphires for Letty and emeralds for Lila.

"To match each of your eyes," she explained. "These are from my favorite jeweler in New York City."

"My heavens, these are far too dear," Lila objected.

"They must have cost a small fortune," Letty added in awe.

They were hardly extravagant, given Papa's means. But she felt a bit ashamed by her family's wealth now that she had witnessed the state of Marchingham Hall and had overheard the dire straits in which Lion—and consequently Letty and Lila—found themselves.

"I wished for a lasting gift," she said simply, "so that you could look upon them and think of your friend back in America."

"As if we could ever forget you," Lila said, tears swimming in her green eyes.

"*Les Trois Mousquetaires*," Letty added on a half sob.

Pain shot through Addy. She would miss her friends. Nothing about her surprise Christmas jaunt to Yorkshire had unfolded as she had planned. She hadn't intended for a snowstorm or for her friends to be absent or to fall in love with Lion. But all of those things had happened.

And now, she needed to do whatever she had to so that she could protect what remained of her broken heart.

# CHAPTER 10

Discreetly, Lion checked his pocket watch. Having house guests was bloody tiresome, and a reminder of why he never had them. Uncle Algernon had cornered him in the orangery some two hours ago, and he didn't show any inclination of slowing down on his long-winded description of the proper cultivation of citrus trees. His uncle was a congenial chap and very caring, but he also scarcely ever ceased talking.

Lion had never met a more garrulous man in his life. He wondered how dear Aunt Helene could possibly bear it. He had already attempted to politely interrupt on no fewer than five separate occasions, and yet Uncle Algernon had swiftly deflected the conversation to yet another subject, continuing a vast discourse on everything from furnaces to politics to orchids to glazing.

Lion needed to escape so that he could at last speak with Addy. Alone.

Enough time had lapsed between the night she had come to his bedroom and this afternoon. He was hoping to propose to her so that they might have a happy announcement for the family on Christmas Day. But he would never be able to do so unless he removed himself from the orangery.

"Oh dear," he interrupted suddenly, seizing his opportunity when Uncle Algernon took a breath. "I nearly forgot that I am meant to be arranging for the cutting of a Christmas tree. My sisters are insisting upon it. If you'll excuse me?"

"Of course," Uncle Algernon said, disappointment lacing his voice. "I'll carry on having a walk about the orangery to look for areas that require improvement."

Dear God. He shuddered to think of how long that particular conversation would take.

Lion forced a smile. "Quite."

Making haste in his retreat, he moved back into the main house, searching every room for Addy. He was met with disappointment at every turn. Addy wasn't in the library, the drawing room, or the music room. He ascended the stairs next, consigning propriety to the devil and going to her bedroom. He had been doing his utmost to follow the rules following the arrival of his sisters, aunt, and uncle, and look at where it had landed him.

Her bedroom door was ajar.

Odd, that. Ordinarily, she kept Dandy inside. Lion knocked and peered in.

"Miss Fox? Dandy?"

He was greeted with silence. The room looked neat and tidy, nary a hint of either Addy or her incorrigible mongrel. Perhaps she was keeping his sisters company. The three of them had been inseparable these past few days.

Frowning, Lion made his way to Lila's chamber, where he knew they had been convening, giggling and making an indecorous amount of noise. He hadn't minded, even if he had been envious of his sisters for having all of Addy's attention.

He rapped on the door. It opened to reveal Lila with tear-stained cheeks and a red nose.

"What is the matter?" he asked, instantly concerned.

"Addy's had to leave," Lila said with a sniff. "She needs to return to New York City."

"Her betrothed, Mr. George Smith, broke his leg when he fell off a horse," Letty added from behind a handkerchief.

She punctuated the announcement by loudly blowing her nose.

Lion stared, struggling to comprehend what his weeping sisters had just said. *Her betrothed. Mr. George Smith. She needs to return to New York City.*

"What the devil?" he blurted out.

"Addy's father sent word that she must return to tend to Mr. Smith," Lila explained, frowning at him as if he were the world's greatest churl.

"Who is Mr. Smith?" he demanded.

"Addy's betrothed," Letty said slowly. "Have you not listened to a word we've said?"

"I've listened, but listening and comprehending are two different beasts entirely," he said grimly. "When did Miss Fox leave?"

"It was easily an hour or two ago," Lila told him. "She came to us, quite distressed, and explained that she and her aunt Pearl needed to go to York so that they wouldn't miss the train to London. Or was it three hours ago?"

"She gave us each the most beautiful pair of earrings for Christmas," Letty added. "Sapphires and emeralds to match our eyes."

"I do wish she hadn't left in such haste. It's not like her."

"She did seem at sixes and sevens. I've never seen her in such a state before."

"I've got to stop her," he said as much to his sisters as to himself.

His mind whirled with these unexpected revelations. Mr. George Smith? Why had she never spoken of the man to him? Why had she given herself to Lion if she already had a betrothed? And why would she leave without at least deigning to tell him goodbye? Only yesterday, she'd expressed an intention to stay beyond Christmas.

None of it made sense.

Lion spun on his heel.

"Lion?" his sisters called after him. "What are you intending?"

"I don't know," he tossed over his shoulder as he stalked to the staircase.

All he *did* know was that he couldn't let Addy go. Not like this.

He rushed to the stables and ordered Athena saddled. Jacob, his head groom, confirmed what his sisters had said, that Addy had left with her aunt, Dandy, and Alfred several hours before. They had taken his carriage, considering that the carriage she had hired for her journey to Marchingham Hall had yet to be repaired. Which meant that not only was she leaving him, but Lion's own blasted grooms and coach had assisted her.

She had a few hours of advantage, and Athena was bred for endurance rather than speed, but Lion was determined. He would find her in York, and he'd have his answers there.

ADDY, Alfred, Aunt Pearl, and Dandy had reached York with just enough time to make passage on the last train leaving to London before Christmas. They were settled in a comfortable private car now, the locomotive rattling down the tracks that were carrying them out of the station. It was something of a miracle they had been able to secure tickets, but when she had realized there was a chance they could leave York today, she had seized it.

Addy stared out the window, trying not to weep as Dandy sat in her lap.

"Are you going to tell me why you suddenly decided to leave Marchingham Hall without warning, and on Christmas Eve, no less?" Aunt Pearl asked quietly.

She had known the question would be coming. Aunt Pearl hadn't made a single query from the moment Addy had arrived, breathless and distraught at her chamber door, until they had settled in the train car.

"I overheard something distressing," she said flatly.

The last few hours had utterly exhausted her. She was equal parts weary and sad, confused and heartbroken.

"Would you like to share what that was?" her aunt asked patiently.

Addy took a deep breath. "It was that Li—the Duke of Marchingham wants to marry me."

"But that's wonderful news, my dear."

"For my dowry," Addy added grimly. "He was speaking with Lady Hargrove in his study, and the door was partially open… I didn't intend to eavesdrop, but when I heard what they were speaking about, I couldn't help myself. It seems that the duke has a great deal of debt and his estates are woefully in need of repair. Marrying me would solve all his problems."

Her voice cracked on the last word.

Dandy licked her chin and then resumed panting, for train rides made her exceedingly nervous. Addy patted her head. At least her loyalty had resumed now that they had left Lion behind.

"Oh my darling Addy," Aunt Pearl said, pity lacing her voice. "I'm so sorry. I know you were harboring tender feelings for the duke."

"I fell in love with him," she admitted, shaking her head. "I know that we were at daggers drawn initially, but over the time we spent at Marchingham Hall, I thought that changed. I thought he saw me differently. I thought I melted his ice away. But I should have known that he was nothing more than a fortune hunter. Why would an elegant, proper duke like Marchingham want a vulgar, troublesome American when he could have his choice of true ladies?"

"Any man would be fortunate to take you as his wife," Aunt Pearl defended her sternly. "Not for your dowry, Addy Louise, but for *you*. You're intelligent and kindhearted and beautiful. I'll not hear another uncivil word about my beloved niece, not even if it comes from her own lips."

Tears stung Addy's eyes anew at her aunt's unflagging loyalty. "This is why you're my favorite aunt."

"I'm your *only* aunt, my dear."

Addy smiled on a half sob. "It's best that you are the only one. No others could possibly compare."

"Did you confront the duke about what you overheard?" Aunt Pearl asked next.

"I couldn't bear to," she confided, feeling foolish for the way she had fled. "My pride and my heart were both dashed to bits. I thought that what we shared meant something to him. Instead, he was just trying to secure his estates."

"Was he familiar with you?"

Aunt Pearl's voice was sharp.

*Bother.* Addy had revealed too much. She averted her gaze out the window.

"It doesn't matter now."

"Adelia Louise, of course it matters. Your mother will have my head when we return if you've been compromised in any way."

She swallowed hard. "Mama doesn't need to know."

"Addy."

Addy heaved a heavy sigh. "I won't tell her, and you aren't to tell her either. I'm not going to be trapped into marriage with a man who only wants me for the wealth I can bring him. I deserve a husband who will love me."

"Yes, my darling, you do," Aunt Pearl agreed quietly. "It is best you waited to tell me all this until after the train left the station, you know."

She glanced back toward her aunt. "Why?"

Aunt Pearl was somber. "Because otherwise, I'd have driven directly back to Marchingham Hall and punched the duke squarely in the eye."

Addy smiled, and then a tear rolled down her cheek when she gave in to another wave of tears as the train took them toward London.

# CHAPTER 11

Finding someone in London when one hadn't the slightest inkling of where that person may have gone was never an easy feat. On Christmas Day, it was nigh impossible. But Lion was determined as he approached yet another hotel in search of Addy.

After racing to York with all haste and inquiring everywhere he could, he had discovered—too late—that Addy, her aunt Pearl, Alfred, and Dandy had boarded the final Christmas Eve train bound for London. He had watched it departing in the distance, carrying her away from him. Dejected, he had turned back to Marchingham Hall, catching up with his empty carriage halfway there.

Fortunately for him, the trains were running on Christmas Day as on Sundays. Which meant that he had managed an early train out of York after wishing his sisters, aunt, and uncle a happy Christmas. Now, he was cold, his shoes and feet were wet from slogging through the streets, and he still had yet to locate Addy. But she was here, somewhere in this vast assortment of streets and buildings.

All he had to do was carry on.

He stopped at the front desk, where an unsmiling young man greeted him with a pointed look at his wet shoes. The establishment was a fine one, and it was true that Lion had tracked rather a lot of grime across the marble entry.

Still, he proffered a slightly soggy calling card. "The Duke of Marchingham looking for Miss Adelia Fox, her maiden aunt companion, and her dog."

For a moment, the gentleman simply stared at Lion, and he feared he would yet again be denied. But then the fellow nodded. "Room fifteen, up the stairs and to your left."

*Finally.*

Addy was here.

Relief surged inside him as he forced a polite smile for the other man's benefit. "Thank you, sir."

Lion crossed the lobby, narrowly avoiding a collision with a matron who had enough feathers on her hat to cover an entire flock of birds, and took the steps two at a time. His feet flew until he reached the correct floor and turned left, following the numbers on doors until he stopped before fifteen.

He had scarcely slept last night, tossing and turning and wondering how the bloody hell he could fix the mess the both of them had made. If she truly had a fiancé, she had a great deal of explaining to do. She was also going to have to throw the poor chap over. Because Lion didn't think he had been wrong about the way Addy felt for him. He knew her well enough to know that she wouldn't have come to him that night if she were in love with someone else.

Whatever had happened to send her fleeing to York and then London, he would have an answer for it. He simply had to. Because he couldn't lose Addy. Not when he had scarcely had her to begin with.

With a deep breath, Lion knocked on the door.

His raps were instantly greeted by loud barks, and he

found himself grinning. That would be Dandy. He'd recognize her anywhere. Fortunately, he had managed to remember to bring pocket cheese.

The door opened a crack. "Who is it?"

Ah, the protective, elder Miss Fox.

"It is Marchingham," he said as a little black snout appeared, poking out of the gap. "Hullo there, Dandy," he said softly, extracting a small hunk of cheese from his pocket and offering it to the hound, who slurped it up eagerly and swallowed it whole.

"You are not welcome here, Your Grace," the elder Miss Fox announced, and closed the door.

He heard whining and scratching on the other side, and he didn't blame Dandy one whit. He felt the same. But he wasn't going anywhere until he spoke with Addy directly. He knocked again, this time with greater insistence.

"Addy?" he called. "Addy, are you in there? I must speak with you."

The door opened, and this time, it was to reveal vibrant green eyes that were red-rimmed and filled with sadness. "Go away, Marchingham."

It was as if someone had landed a blow directly to his midsection. "I'm not going until I can have an audience with you."

"Well, I'm not speaking with you, so you'll have to speak to the door."

She moved to close it, but he wedged his wet shoe on the threshold, keeping her from shutting it. Dandy was there, her brown eyes gazing up at him entreatingly. He removed another small piece of cheese from his waistcoat pocket and offered it to her.

The French bulldog snatched it from his fingers at once.

"Go away, Marchingham," Addy demanded. "And stop attempting to bribe Dandy with pocket cheese."

"I'm not bribing her. She likes me."

Addy's eyes narrowed. "She likes cheese."

"Do you like me, Dandy?" he asked.

Dandy barked obligingly.

"Oh hush, you little traitor," Addy chastised, frowning down at the small dog. "We've had this discussion before."

If he weren't so sick with worry over what was happening, he might have laughed at her antics. Addy Fox was ridiculous, and he loved that about her. In fact, he loved *everything* about her. And that was why he had dashed across England following her, and why he was presently standing at her hotel door with a pocket full of cheddar and sodden shoes.

Well, to be fair, he loved everything about her except for her running away from him without an explanation or even a goodbye. There was the troubling matter of her supposed betrothed, as well.

"We need to talk," Lion told Addy firmly. "If you want me to announce our private affairs to everyone staying on this floor, I shall. But I would prefer not to do so."

She sighed. "I don't think we need to talk."

"Addy, you ran away from me and boarded a train to London without so much as a farewell. I think we have a great deal to talk about."

She stared at him, clearly waging a debate in her own head.

"Don't marry Geoffrey Smith," he said.

Her brow wrinkled. "His name is George, not Geoffrey, and I'm not marrying him."

Relief washed over him. "Then marry me instead."

"I'm not marrying you either, you…you…fortune hunting…*curmudgeon*!"

Her halting insults would have been amusing if not for

two words. *Fortune hunting.* Suddenly, everything made sense.

Lion had believed Addy had run because he hadn't proposed to her in the wake of their night together. When his sisters and aunt and uncle had unceremoniously arrived at Marchingham Hall, he had been admittedly thrown. Uncle Algernon and Aunt Helene had each had his ear, and Addy had tucked herself away in Lila's room for hours upon end. He'd still been struggling with his own feelings, trying to muddle through emotions he'd never thought to feel. He'd thought he had time to propose to her in proper fashion on Christmas Eve.

When she had fled, he had thought he'd misread her, that he had tarried too long and she had grown upset with him. But now, he realized that she must have overheard that blasted uncomfortable conversation with Aunt Helene. His study door had been partially open, and he'd heard a creak.

What a fool he had been.

He wedged his foot deeper into the opening, leaning into her, tantalized by the faintest hint of violets and orris root. It had been only one day, and God how he had missed her.

Lion held her stare. "Let me in so that I may explain."

"What is there to explain? Tell me, did you ever look at me and see just me, or did you look at me and see new carpets and a head gardener and the repairs for a leaky roof?" Fresh tears welled in her eyes as she finished, those verdant orbs turning impossibly greener.

Lion wedged his knee into the gap now. "Addy, when I look at you, I can assure you that carpets and repairs are furthest from my mind. All I see is the most beautiful woman I've ever beheld."

Dandy barked and began pawing at his leg in excitement. He patted her head. He had missed the little scamp as well.

"You're just saying that because you've been caught out," Addy accused, frowning.

He was getting nowhere, still doing his damnedest to get inside the bloody room. Lion sighed. Over his shoulder, he heard the commotion of other guests venturing into the hall, no doubt to see what the fuss was about.

"We're going to start a scandal if you don't let me in," he told her, keeping his voice low.

"I think we've already started a scandal," Addy returned grimly, peering past him into the hall before huffing an irritated sigh. "Very well. You may as well come in. I have no wish for my reputation to be dragged through the mud because you insist upon having an audience with me."

She stepped back so suddenly that Lion nearly lost his footing. He stumbled into the hotel room and closed the door at his back, hoping this wasn't an omen for the dialogue that was about to take place.

Her aunt was eyeing him as if he were a rodent that had scampered across her foot. Dandy, however, had no such reservations. She sat at his feet, gazing up at him adoringly. Lion offered her a bit of pocket cheese as a reward for her adulation. If only Addy were so easily swayed.

"You will find that neither my niece nor I are influenced by cheese," the elder Miss Fox observed acidly, as if she had read his mind.

He cleared his throat. "Madam, I would appreciate a word in private with your niece."

"I think not," Miss Fox said sharply.

Heat crept up his throat. The notion of groveling before Addy's aunt was most unpleasant, but he would do it if he had no other choice.

He turned to Addy, hating her obvious distress. Her sunshine smile was notably absent, and she looked as if she had been weeping. Knowing he was the cause for her upset made his gut churn.

"You overheard some of the conversation between myself and Aunt Helene," he said.

Her chin went up. "I heard all of it that I needed to hear."

"I think not." Lion thought of the moment he'd heard a sound in the hall during his tête-à-tête with his aunt before dismissing it as nothing. "You heard only the beginning. You left before you heard the most important part."

"What was that?" she asked, her tone guarded. "That you require a new carriage or that your town house needs to be fitted for electricity? That you must have a new wardrobe?"

"No." He looked deeply into her eyes, willing her to believe him. "That I've fallen in love with you."

Her lips parted, and she stared at him in silent shock.

It was as he had suspected, then. She had overheard part of his conversation with Aunt Helene, who had been far too concerned about Addy being an heiress.

He reached for her hands, gratified when she didn't immediately snatch them away, and continued. "What you heard wasn't wrong. I am woefully impoverished. My estates are in dire need of funds and repair. The carpets are threadbare, I've had to sell off priceless paintings to pay the creditors, and my sisters have been wearing outmoded gowns for three years. I spent more than I could afford on tuition for the Académie Clairemont in the hope that they might acquire the éclat necessary to secure good husbands and futures for themselves. We know how that ended."

Addy bit her lip. "If you still hold me responsible for Lila and Letty being removed from finishing school—"

"I don't," he interrupted gently. "It was easy to blame you before I knew you. I was angry with my sisters and frustrated. I had no notion how to launch them in Society when they were of age, and I was mired by debt from my father and grandfather before him, weighed down by the burden of so much obligation... It was making me miserable, Addy. Until you came along. You with your dazzling smiles and ridiculous radiance, your utter lack of propriety and your stubborn defiance. And Dandy with her happy bouts and loud barks and penchant for eating ears. The both of you have made me happy for the first time in a very long time."

Addy laughed and hiccupped at the same time, rather proving his point. She was irresistible. Utterly without artifice. And he loved her all the more for it.

"To be fair, Dandy has never *eaten* an ear," Addy pointed out. "She licks them and gives the occasional nibble."

Dandy, apparently tired of not being fawned upon or gifted cheese, barked and then began having a happy bout, racing from one end of the room to the other, sliding on the hardwood floor and slamming into plaster with her side before turning and running back again in a black blur of uninhibited motion.

"Your dog is mad," he pointed out.

"She is merely enthusiastic," Addy defended.

He wanted to kiss her so badly that it was an ache he felt all the way to the soles of his feet. But Lion was acutely aware of her aunt, hovering on the periphery, watching them sternly behind her gold-rimmed spectacles.

"Addy, I don't care that you're an heiress. I am a poor man, but I am also a man who is determined. I can sell off more paintings and some of the estates. I am working with my steward to make the farms more efficient and profitable. I will happily eschew your fortune. Your father may keep all his wealth. I don't want it. All I want is you."

"But you were agreeing with your aunt," Addy protested. "I heard you. And you disapprove of me."

"Aunt Helene, like Uncle Algernon, has good intentions, but she also loves to hear the sound of her own voice. I didn't care to tell her the details of our private relationship, so I was merely agreeing. When she pressed the matter, I made my feelings for you clear, however. My greatest regret is that I didn't tell you first. I should have done so, and I am sorry for that. I should have told you that night, but I…"

*Bloody hell.*

Lion stopped himself from finishing what he'd been about to say, casting an uneasy glance in her aunt's direction.

The elder Miss Fox was eyeing him in a considering fashion. "I think I will meander downstairs to take some tea. I'll be back in half an hour. And if anything untoward occurs while I'm gone or if you make my niece cry again, be forewarned, Your Grace. I've been known to blacken a man's eye in my day."

Lion didn't think Aunt Pearl had much of a chance of doing him bodily harm, but he didn't say so. She was protective of Addy, and that was all that mattered.

He inclined his head. "Thank you."

She looked to her niece. "Addy, dear?"

Addy nodded. "You may go, Aunt Pearl. I'll be fine with Li—with His Grace."

Her aunt's lips twitched, and she raised a brow. "Half an hour."

She didn't say anything else before she quietly quit the room. Dandy, who had finished her happy bout and exhausted herself, now lolled on her side, panting. Lion felt a surge of powerful emotion within his chest, an unrelenting sense of rightness. This was where he was meant to be, with Addy, with Dandy. He knew it to his marrow.

"Do you mean it?" Addy asked him, stealing his attention again.

"I meant every word I said to you," he told her fervently.

She bit her lower lip. "But especially the part where you said you love me. Do you mean that?"

"God, yes." He lowered his head and pressed his forehead to hers. "I love you, Adelia Louise Fox. You, not your dowry. Just *you*."

Dandy trotted back over to them and pawed at his leg.

Lion glanced down, amused. "And you as well, mongrel."

"Dandy isn't a mongrel."

"I know." He couldn't hide his grin. "She's your darling."

"And she's never sleeping in the stables."

"I wouldn't dream of making her."

"And what about my dowry?"

"It's yours to do with as you like. The marriage contract will be written as such, should you do me the honor of agreeing to become my duchess."

"You truly don't care about my father's fortune?" she breathed.

"I'm sorry you overheard the worst part of that bloody conversation. All I can promise is that I'll live each day of our lives proving just how much I love you."

"And Dandy."

He chuckled. "And Dandy."

She squeezed his hands. "Lion?"

"Yes, darling?"

"I love you too."

His heart soared, a joy so profound that it momentarily robbed him of speech exploding within. He kissed her then, because he couldn't go on another moment without knowing her lips beneath his. She loved him. Addy loved him. He'd been too afraid to hope, moving through the last day like an automaton.

He ended the kiss, needing to hear the rest. "Will you do me the greatest honor of marrying me, Adelia Louise Fox?"

"You know, when you call me Adelia Louise, I don't mind it nearly as much as I do when Aunt Pearl does," she teased.

This woman.

"Addy," he prodded.

A grin broke over her face. "Yes, I will marry you, Lionel Hawthorne."

"Thank God." He kissed her swiftly and released her hands, pulling her into his embrace.

When they were both breathless, he lifted his head, gazing down at the woman who had stolen his heart—his wild American hoyden, so perfect for him in every way.

"Merry Christmas," she said softly, smiling at him.

*Christmas.* He hadn't a gift for her. He hadn't a tree. They were in London at a hotel, where neither of them had intended to be. What a mess he'd made of it all.

"I'm sorry I ruined Christmas," he told her earnestly. "I'll make it up to you, darling. I swear it."

She cupped his cheek. "You didn't ruin it, Lion. This is the best Christmas I've ever known."

Dandy pawed at his leg, but he ignored her, all his attention upon her mama instead.

He kissed Addy again, smiling against her lips. "Yet."

# EPILOGUE

## OCEAN CITY, MD

*July 1886*

"It's insufferably hot," Lion grumbled, "and I'm reasonably certain I spied a mosquito earlier that was the size of my head."

Addy gave him a playful swat on the arm. "Oh, do stop fussing. It's the midst of July. Surely you didn't expect it to be cold here in the summer."

Beyond them, the ocean rhythmically crashed on the shore and seagulls called overhead. They sat on the covered porch of the cottage her father had gifted them—one of many wedding gifts, all of which had been woefully extravagant, in true Cornelius Fox fashion. Ocean City was a relatively newly incorporated town situated on the beautiful beaches of the Maryland coast. Her father had invested in it a decade earlier, purchasing property as he so often did, along with building a towering hotel that had been recently constructed.

She and Lion had decided to honeymoon here for a month, taking the rail from New York City through Pennsylvania and Delaware. A ferry had brought them across a placid bay, the sun glinting off the waters, and Addy had breathed deeply of the salt air, taking in the rugged beauty of the surrounding land with its pine trees and white sand.

Dandy had stayed behind in the city with Aunt Pearl to watch over her, and although Addy missed her beloved companion, she was grateful for the time to devote solely to her new husband. Even if he was grumbling about the weather and the mosquitoes.

"Does the sun ever cease shining?" he asked wryly.

She waved her fan at him. "I hope not. I adore it."

"What I wouldn't give for a snowball fight." He sighed wistfully.

Addy chuckled. "I can best you at a snowball fight any day."

"I shall demand a rematch when we are back at Marchingham Hall this Christmas."

"With pleasure."

They had married in New York City before their families and friends and the cream of high Society. The latter had been Mama's doing, of course. She had been overjoyed to see her daughter marrying a duke, and no expense had been spared. Addy had allowed her mother to run wild with her plotting and planning. She hadn't cared about the dress or the flowers or who was invited. All she had cared about was that she was marrying the man she loved and that her best friends in all the world, Lila and Letty, were now her sisters in truth.

The plan was to honeymoon at the Ocean City cottage for a month, followed by a trip back to New York City before Addy, Lion, and Dandy returned to England and spent some time settling into Marchingham Hall. True to his word, Lion had made certain that the vast funds settled upon Addy at their wedding remained hers. But she had already determined that they would restore his estates together. She was more than happy to see her dowry put to good use.

"This is a beautiful place," Lion admitted at her side. "I will own that whilst I didn't expect it to be quite so hot, I can well see the allure. The seaside is magnificent."

"It *is* magnificent," Addy agreed softly, but it wasn't the Atlantic Ocean that was captivating her at the moment.

Rather, it was him.

The breeze was ruffling his burnished-gold waves, and he hadn't shaved that morning, leaving the glint of whiskers on his angular jaw. He turned to her, his icy-blue gaze darkening as their stares clashed and held.

"Do you know, I think I've heard of a cure for the Maryland heat," she told him, a wicked idea flaring to life.

He raised a brow, looking ducal and irresistible all at once. "Oh?"

"Yes." She rose from her chair, moving toward the cottage's front door. "It involves the removal of all one's clothing."

Lion was out of his seat as well, following in her wake. "I think we should give it a try, my love."

They made it through the door giggling like children, and then they were in each other's arms, kissing and tearing at their garments. His mouth was hot and possessive on hers, and he tasted like the lemonade they had been sipping on the porch, sweet and tart. They kicked off their shoes. She moaned and undid the buttons on his waistcoat before moving to his shirt. Lion unhooked her bodice and untied her skirt.

A path of discarded clothes trailed behind them as they burst into their bedroom. Her corset and drawers and his shirt fell away. Stockings came next. Finally, his trousers. But when she reached for his cock, rigid and ready, Lion scooped her into his arms instead.

Addy made a startled sound, wrapping her arms around his neck as he gently deposited her on the mattress. She had a moment to admire his lean, muscled form before he settled on the bed at her feet.

"I've heard of another cure as well," he murmured, caressing her.

"Oh?" she asked breathlessly, opening herself to him.

"Mmm." Lion's big hands glided up her inner thighs, his gaze hot on the flesh that had been revealed to him. "Licking one's wife's cunny."

A different kind of heat arced through her at his wicked words. Lion had a deliciously naughty side she'd only just begun to experience now that they were husband and wife. Hearing his proper aristocratic voice utter vulgarities was havoc upon her ability to resist him.

So she didn't even try.

"That sounds like an excellent cure," she breathed as he lowered his head and pressed a kiss to her sex.

His tongue swiped lovingly over her pearl. "The best."

Lion hooked her legs over his shoulders and cupped her bottom, pulling her to him as if she were a feast he intended to devour. Her head rolled back into the pile of feather pillows, luxuriating in the pleasure of his mouth on her, the sea breeze wafting gently through the open windows, the sunlight glinting in his hair.

He sucked and nipped at her, and she moaned. "Lion."

"My love." He licked her seam, then found her entrance.

Oh, dear heavens. The slick glide of his tongue slipping deep inside her was nothing short of glorious. Splendid. Incredible.

*I am going to run out of words*, she thought weakly as bliss danced up her spine.

"You don't need words," he murmured against her. "Just feel."

Had she said that aloud, then? Apparently so. But it didn't matter. She was more than happy to obey her husband—at least in this regard—and to surrender herself to the mindless pleasure he was visiting upon her.

And oh, what pleasure it was. He licked, sucked, nibbled. Just when she thought she couldn't withstand any more, he gently flicked his tongue over her bud, wringing new sensations from her as he sank two fingers into her. Each deliberate swirl of his tongue took her higher, building the pressure in her core as he thrust in and out.

With a cry, she came undone, her orgasm washing over her with as much force as the waves of the ocean. Lion's mouth remained fastened upon her as he somehow worked a second orgasm from her, lapping up her spend and suckling her sensitized nub before he finally rose, aligning his body with hers.

"You were right about a cure for the heat," he murmured as he rained kisses on her breasts, simultaneously slicking his thick cock in her wetness. "I suggest we remain naked for the rest of the day, and perhaps tomorrow as well."

She threaded her fingers through his hair, arching her back when he sucked a nipple into his hot mouth. "How about for the rest of our honeymoon?"

He released her nipple and grinned at her, a lock of hair falling rakishly over his brow. "Perfect notion."

"I am generally quite perfect in all ways," she teased breathlessly, thinking him impossibly handsome. "It is a universally acknowledged truth on both sides of the Atlantic Ocean, you know."

He flexed his hips and sank deep inside her in one delicious thrust, filling her. He groaned.

"I know, darling," he rasped. "I know."

He began to move, sending pure ecstasy careening through her, and Addy held him tightly as they made love to the rhythm of the waves pounding on the beach.

THANK you so very much for reading *The Duke Who Ruined Christmas*! I hope you consider this book a warm holiday hug from me to you. I loved every moment of writing Lion and Addy's (and Dandy's!) festive happily ever after. For a bit of history, check out my Author's Note.

Please stay in touch! The only way to be sure you'll know what's next from me is to sign up for my newsletter here: http://eepurl.com/dyJSar. Please join my reader group for early excerpts, cover reveals, and more here: https://www.facebook.com/groups/scarlettscottreaders. And if you're in the mood to chat all things steamy historical romance and read a different book together each month, join my book club, Dukes Do It Hotter right here: https://www.facebook.com/groups/hotdukes because we're having a whole lot of fun!

# AUTHOR'S HISTORICAL NOTE

The French bulldog breed was officially recognized by the AKC in 1898, but it began well before that in England before shifting to France. In Paris, the breed became very popular, and they even feature in Impressionist paintings of the era. By the late 1800s, French bulldogs became popular with high society Americans too, just like Addy.

Ocean City, Maryland is a place that is near and dear to my heart, and I'm thrilled that I've finally managed to work it into a book. According to my research, Ocean City was incorporated in 1875, and by the time Lion and Addy honeymooned there, it was already becoming a popular coastal holiday destination, complete with a hotel and an elevated boardwalk. It felt like the perfect place for them to begin their happily ever after.

# DON'T MISS SCARLETT'S OTHER ROMANCES!

## Complete Book List
**HISTORICAL ROMANCE**

Heart's Temptation
A Mad Passion (Book One)
Rebel Love (Book Two)
Reckless Need (Book Three)
Sweet Scandal (Book Four)
Restless Rake (Book Five)
Darling Duke (Book Six)
The Night Before Scandal (Book Seven)

Wicked Husbands
Her Errant Earl (Book One)
Her Lovestruck Lord (Book Two)
Her Reformed Rake (Book Three)
Her Deceptive Duke (Book Four)
Her Missing Marquess (Book Five)
Her Virtuous Viscount (Book Six)

DON'T MISS SCARLETT'S OTHER ROMANCES!

Wicked Dukes Society
Duke with a Reputation (Book One)
Duke with a Debt (Book Two)
Duke with a Secret (Book Three)
Duke with a Lie (Book Four)

Christmas Dukes
The Duke Who Despised Christmas (Book One)
The Duke Who Ruined Christmas (Book Two)

League of Dukes
Nobody's Duke (Book One)
Heartless Duke (Book Two)
Dangerous Duke (Book Three)
Shameless Duke (Book Four)
Scandalous Duke (Book Five)
Fearless Duke (Book Six)

Notorious Ladies of London
Lady Ruthless (Book One)
Lady Wallflower (Book Two)
Lady Reckless (Book Three)
Lady Wicked (Book Four)
Lady Lawless (Book Five)
Lady Brazen (Book 6)

Unexpected Lords
The Detective Duke (Book One)
The Playboy Peer (Book Two)
The Millionaire Marquess (Book Three)
The Goodbye Governess (Book Four)

Dukes Most Wanted
Forever Her Duke (Book One)

DON'T MISS SCARLETT'S OTHER ROMANCES!

Forever Her Marquess (Book Two)
Forever Her Rake (Book Three)
Forever Her Earl (Book Four)
Forever Her Viscount (Book Five)
Forever Her Scot (Book Six)

The Wicked Winters
Wicked in Winter (Book One)
Wedded in Winter (Book Two)
Wanton in Winter (Book Three)
Wishes in Winter (Book 3.5)
Willful in Winter (Book Four)
Wagered in Winter (Book Five)
Wild in Winter (Book Six)
Wooed in Winter (Book Seven)
Winter's Wallflower (Book Eight)
Winter's Woman (Book Nine)
Winter's Whispers (Book Ten)
Winter's Waltz (Book Eleven)
Winter's Widow (Book Twelve)
Winter's Warrior (Book Thirteen)
A Merry Wicked Winter (Book Fourteen)

The Sinful Suttons
Sutton's Spinster (Book One)
Sutton's Sins (Book Two)
Sutton's Surrender (Book Three)
Sutton's Seduction (Book Four)
Sutton's Scoundrel (Book Five)
Sutton's Scandal (Book Six)
Sutton's Secrets (Book Seven)

Rogue's Guild
Her Ruthless Duke (Book One)

DON'T MISS SCARLETT'S OTHER ROMANCES!

Her Dangerous Beast (Book Two)
Her Wicked Rogue (Book 3)

Royals and Renegades
How to Love a Dangerous Rogue (Book One)
How to Tame a Dissolute Prince (Book Two)

Sins and Scoundrels
Duke of Depravity
Prince of Persuasion
Marquess of Mayhem
Sarah
Earl of Every Sin
Duke of Debauchery
Viscount of Villainy

Sins and Scoundrels Box Set Collections
Volume 1
Volume 2

The Wicked Winters Box Set Collections
Collection 1
Collection 2
Collection 3
Collection 4

Wicked Husbands Box Set Collections
Volume 1
Volume 2

Notorious Ladies of London Box Set Collections
Volume 1
Volume 2

DON'T MISS SCARLETT'S OTHER ROMANCES!

The Sinful Suttons Box Set Collections
Volume 1
Volume 2

Stand-alone Novella
Lord of Pirates

**CONTEMPORARY ROMANCE**
Love's Second Chance
Reprieve (Book One)
Perfect Persuasion (Book Two)
Win My Love (Book Three)

Coastal Heat
Loved Up (Book One)

**Writing as Lora Whitney**

**Mafia Romance**
Andriani Brothers
Brutal Devil (Book One)

## ABOUT THE AUTHOR

*USA Today* and Amazon bestselling author Scarlett Scott™ writes steamy Victorian and Regency romance with strong, intelligent heroines and sexy alpha heroes. She lives in Pennsylvania and Maryland with her Canadian husband, their adorable identical twins, a demanding diva of a dog, and a zany cat who showed up one summer and never left.

A self-professed literary junkie and nerd, she loves reading anything, but especially romance novels and poetry. Catch up with her on her website https://scarlettscottauthor.com. Hearing from readers never fails to make her day.

Scarlett's complete book list and information about upcoming releases can be found at https://scarlettscottauthor.com.

Connect with Scarlett! You can find her here:
Join Scarlett Scott's reader group on Facebook for early excerpts, giveaways, and a whole lot of fun!
Sign up for her newsletter here
https://www.tiktok.com/@authorscarlettscott

- facebook.com/AuthorScarlettScott
- x.com/scarscoromance
- instagram.com/scarlettscottauthor
- bookbub.com/authors/scarlett-scott
- amazon.com/Scarlett-Scott/e/B004NW8N2I
- pinterest.com/scarlettscott

Printed in Dunstable, United Kingdom